SPECIAL MESSAGE TO READERS

THE ULVERSCROFT FOUNDATION
(registered UK charity number 264873)
was established in 1972 to provide funds for
research, diagnosis and treatment of eye diseases.
Examples of major projects funded by
the Ulverscroft Foundation are:-

- The Children's Eye Unit at Moorfields Eye Hospital, London
- The Ulverscroft Children's Eye Unit at Great Ormond Street Hospital for Sick Children
- Funding research into eye diseases and treatment at the Department of Ophthalmology, University of Leicester
- The Ulverscroft Vision Research Group, Institute of Child Health
- Twin operating theatres at the Western Ophthalmic Hospital, London
- The Chair of Ophthalmology at the Royal Australian College of Ophthalmologists

You can help further the work of the Foundation
by making a donation or leaving a legacy.
Every contribution is gratefully received. If you
would like to help support the Foundation or
require further information, please contact:

THE ULVERSCROFT FOUNDATION
The Green, Bradgate Road, Anstey
Leicester LE7 7FU, England
Tel: (0116) 236 4325

website: www.foundation.ulverscroft.com

THE DANCE OF LOVE

Starting a new phase in her life after the death of her chronically ill mother, Carrie decides to go on a cruise to Alaska. All the other passengers seem to be in couples, though, and she immediately feels left out. Then she meets fellow lone passenger Tom, who becomes a firm friend — until the handsome and elusive Greg steals her heart. Should Carrie take a chance on him, or accept the security offered by Tom? And what will happen when the cruise comes to an end?

JEAN ROBINSON

---◆---

THE DANCE
OF LOVE

Complete and Unabridged

LINFORD
Leicester

First published in Great Britain in 2017

First Linford Edition
published 2017

A catalogue record for this book is available
from the British Library.

ISBN 978–1–4448–3150–4

Published by
F. A. Thorpe (Publishing)
Anstey, Leicestershire

Set by Words & Graphics Ltd.
Anstey, Leicestershire
Printed and bound in Great Britain by
T. J. International Ltd., Padstow, Cornwall

This book is printed on acid-free paper

1

All Aboard

'Hello, dear. Husband deserted you, has he?'

The plump little woman with grey frizzed hair plonked herself down on a chair beside Carrie. Tables in the ship's restaurant were filling as passengers brought food from the buffet. Carrie smiled and edged her seat a little further away.

'I'm Annie. What's your name, dear?' Annie didn't wait for an answer before taking a bite of her sausage roll and then launching forth again. 'My George always makes a beeline for the bar. Can't do with this bubbly. I expect yours is the same.'

Carrie took a gulp of the champagne she'd been handed on her way into the restaurant. 'No, I don't have anyone with me,' she said, trying to sound confident.

'Oh, I see.' Annie gave her a questioning look. 'That's very brave of you, dear, coming on a cruise all on your own.' She leaned forward and placed a hand over Carrie's. 'Well, now, you come and find me if you want anything. This is my fifth cruise, so I pretty much know my way round.'

Carrie thanked her, finished her champagne as quickly as she could, and told Annie she wanted to find her cabin and get unpacked.

'But you haven't touched your food,' Annie said, a look of concern on her face.

Carrie smiled weakly. 'I'm really not hungry.'

Annie frowned. 'You youngsters, you don't eat nearly enough.'

'I'll make up for it at dinner,' Carrie said as she watched Annie demolish a dainty ham sandwich in two bites.

Once alone in her cabin, Carrie relaxed. This cruise had seemed such an adventure when she'd seen it advertised in the magazine all those months ago. They were travelling on the *Flora May* from Vancouver up through the mountains and fjords of Alaska, towards the land of the midnight sun. The holiday brochure had shown romantic views of people lounging on deck surrounded by white rails turned mellow in the setting sun. She'd rushed out to the travel agent's and booked up before she'd had time to have second thoughts. For the first time since her mum had died, she had felt a spark of life stir in her.

But when she'd stood on the quayside early this morning, staring up at the towering side of this huge cruise liner gleaming white in the June sunshine, a lonely fear had gripped her.

With all the other passengers, she had traipsed up the gangway and then towards the smartly dressed stewards, who had directed them to a welcome lunch. Long tables round the room had held an array of most tempting dishes, but Carrie had no appetite. She'd put a small amount on her plate only because it was what everyone else was doing. Sitting alone at one of the tables, it had seemed that every eye was on her, and she'd wished she could have been anywhere but in the centre of this mass of happy, chattering people. Then Annie had joined her and the panic had lessened. But Annie was only passing time while her husband was in the bar. Carrie had no husband about to join her. What had she been thinking when, all those months ago, this holiday seemed like such a good idea?

Looking round her cabin now, she smiled with satisfaction. It was tiny, but the best she could afford. The apartments on the upper decks were well out of her league. Still, it was neat and comfortable, with a window looking out onto open deck. A chair stood at a small dressing table, and there was an alcove for hanging clothes. She peered into the shower compartment. It was clean and functional. The narrow bed up against the wall was fine, too. She was used to small spaces. Her home was a tiny cottage in a Cotswold village, the home she'd shared with her invalid mum. Now it was hers alone.

There was a knock at the door, and when she opened it a little Indonesian man in a white tunic top and black trousers grinned at her. In broken English he introduced himself as her steward for the week and asked if there was anything she required. His friendly manner had her smiling and, as she closed the door, the excitement she'd felt when getting on the plane began to bubble up again.

The flight from Heathrow had been fine. She'd managed to get a window seat on the coach from the airport to the hotel in Vancouver, where they had spent a couple of days before joining the cruise ship. She'd loved Vancouver: wandering along the beach at sunset, watching young people sitting round on the sand lighting barbeques. She'd bought fish and chips one night and eaten them whilst perched on an old log, listening to a group strumming guitars and singing as the sun sank low towards the sea.

It was only once she had boarded this ship that Carrie had realised she was all alone. Alone among this horde of people for a whole week. And there was no escape.

She heaved her suitcase onto the bed, determined not to be intimidated. This was to be the holiday of a lifetime. There was no way she'd ever be able to afford anything like it again. As soon as she got home she'd be working, and holidays after that would be few and far between. Nothing was going to stop her enjoying this one.

And she had her little cabin as a retreat if she needed it, somewhere she could be alone for a while. But mostly she was going to get out there and experience everything the cruise had to offer. And there was no time like the present to start. With a spring in her step, she set off in search of the lift. Unpacking could be done later. Getting her bearings on this huge vessel was her first priority.

A sign on the promenade deck said that three laps round it would clock up a mile. That might come in useful if the food on offer for lunch was anything to go by. The lift had a whole panel of buttons. She pressed the one for deck ten. Might as well start at the top.

Here a huge observatory with great expanses of glass gave a panoramic view across the harbour to distant mountains and above, through the glass roof, to a perfect azure-blue sky. White-coated waiters were serving drinks to a scattering of passengers sitting chatting round rattan tables amidst potted palms. Musicians played softly on a raised platform in one corner. A few heads turned as Carrie stood there, which made her feel exposed. She quickly found her way back to the lift, wondering yet again how she was ever going to fit in.

As she wandered through the ship, examining every part with delight, calm was restored. It was mostly art nouveau, all smooth cream curves with exquisite touches of gold, giving a feel of relaxed elegance. Floral arrangements were set into alcoves. A tall lamp in a dark corner illuminated a leopard-skin couch. There were intimate little bars, one with blue leather-topped stools and concealed lighting that made the glasses beneath it sparkle. The barman smiled at Carrie. She gave a nervous smile back and quickly moved on.

A sweeping staircase carpeted in lush red stopped her in her tracks. As she stared up at the oil paintings and statues at the curve, she sensed someone was standing behind her.

'Impressive, isn't it?'

She turned to see a man of medium height with balding hair and a pleasant face. 'I didn't expect it to be like this,' she admitted.

'No, it's quite an eye-opener.'

She liked his easy manner and soft voice. His smile relaxed her.

He extended his hand. 'Tom Maxwell,' he said, looking directly at her.

'Carrie Davis,' she said, taking his hand and smiling.

They stood discussing the paintings, mostly of ships in stormy seas, then he wandered off. Something about the encounter lifted Carrie's spirits, and she continued with a lighter step until she was back in her cabin.

While she was arranging her dresses on the rail, the alarm went and she remembered they were to have a mandatory lifeboat drill. Pulling her lifejacket from the shelf above, she began to struggle into it as she hurried down the alleyways in the direction she'd been told to go.

It wasn't difficult finding the correct lifeboat station, as there were stewards at every turn giving directions. The whole thing had an air of excitement about it, with people rushing along trailing lifejackets and laughing as they attempted to fasten them on.

Tom was standing beside one of the

lifeboats tying his lifejacket in place, and beckoned Carrie over. Once they had them secured, they watched others struggling with tangled straps and were both soon laughing together. Officers moving along the line ticked off names. Everyone seemed in good humour, and there was a lot of joking as they eventually got it all sorted.

'Are you here on your own?' Tom asked. Then he pulled a face as if to say, *Sorry I shouldn't have asked that.*

Carrie smiled. 'Yes, I'm alone. How about you?'

He gave a resigned smile and shrugged. 'Afraid so. Sometimes you just have to get on with it, don't you?'

'I didn't expect to feel so lonely,' Carrie said, then winced and wondered what had made her say such a thing to a complete stranger. Except that he didn't feel like a stranger.

He was studying her.

'Sorry, I'm just being silly,' she mumbled, looking away in embarrassment as tears threatened.

'Hey, don't feel like that,' he said. 'I wish I'd spoken to you earlier when we were on the coach coming from the airport. We could have sat together. I wasn't sure if you were on your own or with those ladies.'

She looked up into his pale blue eyes and saw a kind man, one she felt she could trust. 'No, they were just three ladies travelling together. The one sharing my seat spent all her time leaning over talking across the aisle to her friends. It seemed like she hadn't noticed I was there.'

'That wasn't very friendly. I had a seat to myself. You could have joined me,' Tom said.

'I didn't mind at all. There was such a lot to see. I was quite content looking out of the window.'

'Tell you what — when this malarkey's finished, we'll go to one of the bars and have a drink. Get to know each other.'

Carrie gave him a warm smile. 'Well, there are plenty to choose from. I think

I counted eight on my ramblings this afternoon.'

'And we have to sample them all. That's one a day for the cruise.'

'Yes, I think I can cope with that.' She began to feel quite light-hearted at the thought of having someone to have a drink with.

She took her lifejacket back to her cabin and changed into a flowery summer dress and sandals, then managed to find the Oyster Bar where she'd arranged to meet Tom. He was sitting at a tall round table near one of the windows with a view across the harbour towards the mountains. Fishing nets and oyster pots adorned the walls. In one corner a group of musicians were playing sea shanties. Tom got up when he saw her and pulled out a chair so that she could sit opposite to him.

'How do you fancy a cocktail to start the holiday?' he said, picking up the drinks menu and handing it to her.

She glanced at the list and began to giggle as she read out the names.

'Totem Pole Delight, Gold Digger's Punch. Think I'll stick with a gin and tonic. At least I know what I'm getting then.'

He gave a mock frown. 'That's not very adventurous. Come on, now, let's live dangerously.'

'Okay, you choose.' She was in such a happy mood she would try anything.

A waiter in crisp white shirt and black waistcoat came over to take their order. Tom looked at Carrie uncertainly. 'You won't be mad with me if you don't like it, will you?'

'Of course I will.' It was good to have this light-hearted banter. Life had been too serious for too long.

The drinks were exotic, with fruit and straws sticking out of the top. Carrie took a sip of hers and decided she liked it. Tom pulled a face and they were laughing again.

While they sipped their drinks, Tom told her he was a social worker in a deprived area of Liverpool but loved his job and found it challenging. His wife had died three years ago, and now he lived on his own and took off every holiday on a different adventure.

Carrie told him she had looked after her mother for the past three years after a stroke had confined her to a wheelchair, and how she'd booked this holiday on the spur of the moment just after her mum had died. 'She used to love looking through holiday brochures; said it was the next best thing to being there. She'd always wanted to travel but never had the chance.'

'So you decided you would,' Tom added.

Carrie nodded. 'I thought I'd do it while I had the chance. My mum had a small insurance policy. She told me that when she died she wanted me to use it to travel. As soon as I saw this holiday advertised, I knew it was what I wanted to do: the icy fjords, the stark mountains, blue-green water. When I get home I have to start working again.'

'And you're a dancer,' he finished for her.

She stared at him. 'How did you know that?'

He shrugged. 'I can tell by the way you walk, the way you hold your head. You have the poise of a dancer. I can just see you on stage, hair in a bun, nose in the air, pirouetting in a lovely floaty dress.'

She gave an embarrassed laugh. 'More like teaching a waltz in a church hall to people with two left feet.'

He raised an eyebrow. 'I think you could do more than that.'

She shrugged. 'I was a professional dancer; spent most of my teenage years taking dancing exams. My partner and I entered competitions and danced all over the country.'

'And this partner?' he asked when she paused.

She swallowed hard. 'We were going to be married and start up a dancing school. Then my mum became ill.' She could hear the tremble in her own voice.

Quietly he watched as she slowly

gained her composure and gave him a weak smile. 'They're sailing soon and there's a party on the pool deck. It should be fun,' he said gently.

Carrie shrugged and felt her smile slipping again. 'I'm not sure I'm in party mood.'

Tom stood up, pushed his chair back and reached out to take her hand. 'You will be when we get there. Go and put on your glad rags and I'll see you in half an hour.'

This time the smile came naturally. 'How can I refuse?'

'You can't.'

★ ★ ★

The large area of deck where the sailing party was now in full swing was flooded with early-evening sunshine, decorated with bunting and bustling with excited people drinking and laughing as they watched the land slipping by. Carrie stood nervously at the edge, trying to summon the courage to plunge in amongst the crowd. A deck bar was busy serving drinks as people milled round and chatted in groups. The Malayan barman in a tropical shirt was shaking a cocktail. Two elderly ladies stood watching as a pretty barmaid smiled whilst pouring their drinks. White railed steps led from an upper deck, down which more and more people were coming to join the party. Others were viewing the proceedings from above, the stark white of the ship now mellowed in the evening light.

They were sailing through calm waters, distant mountains dark against the pale blue sky. A lonely fear suddenly spread through Carrie. Then Tom was at her side, and the feeling passed. Dressed in an open-necked shirt and light trousers, he looked very much in holiday mood, and was holding two tall glasses of something fruity with flags and straws sticking out of the top.

He handed one to Carrie with a chortle. 'Not sure if I wanted another fruit cocktail, but it seems the thing to have.'

She took it with a smile. 'You know what they say about when in Rome.'

'And I firmly believe in it,' Tom said. 'That's what we come on holiday for, isn't it?'

'Absolutely. I want to experience everything I can on this cruise.'

'Me, too.'

They managed to ease themselves through the crowd towards the stern of the ship, and stood side by side watching the sun dip in a cloudless sky, the steady motion of the ship leaving a trail of sea foam in its wake. A light breeze freshened the air. Blues music played gently in the background. Peace settled on deck as people found their friends and began to chat quietly and absorb the atmosphere.

Tom turned to Carrie. 'I like your dress. Red suits you.'

Carrie felt her colour rising, but it was a good feeling. It had been a long time since a man had paid her a compliment. She'd loved this strappy cocktail dress when she'd bought it, the close-fitting style and the way it skimmed her hips and flared out round her knees.

'I'm so glad we found each other,' Tom said.

She gave him a shy smile. 'Me, too.'

They stayed out on deck until it was time to go in to dinner. Tom kept her close at his side as he escorted her through the ship towards the restaurant.

'I've managed to arrange for us to sit at the same table,' he said. 'Caused some consternation amongst the stewards, but they sorted it eventually.' Then he gave Carrie an uncertain look. 'I hope you don't mind. I thought it would be nice to sit together.'

Carrie beamed at him as they joined the queue waiting to be seated. 'I'm delighted. I was dreading being stuck at a table with other couples and being asked awkward questions about being on my own.'

Her first glimpse of the restaurant almost took her breath away: it was huge. Starched white linen covered chairs and tables, and rows of gleaming silver cutlery and crystal wine goblets glinted in the light from sparkling chandeliers that lit up the ivory walls and ceiling. Most of the men wore suits, their ladies glammed up with neatly styled hair and expensive jewellery. A fountain played in one corner, and the centre column was decorated with bowls of exotic fruits nestled on blocks of sculptured ice. Waiters in starched white jackets with lots of gold braid were guiding people to their tables, pulling out chairs and flicking table napkins. Carrie had never encountered anything so grand in her life, and she kept close to Tom when their turn came to be shown to their seats.

His hand on her back as they followed the waiter was comforting. It made her feel safe. He waited for her to take her seat, then whispered so that only she could hear: 'You are the most beautiful woman here.'

She noticed the others at the table looking at them and feared they had heard what Tom had said. But they were just smiling in a welcoming way, and her nerves settled.

Jackie introduced herself first. She was a big-boned young woman with a mop of dark brown hair and a broad smile that immediately put Carrie at her ease. Justin, her husband, was a tall, pleasant young man with short cropped hair and a fresh complexion. They seemed to dominate the conversation and soon had everyone chatting. Eve and Harry were on honeymoon and, when not looking into each other's eyes, seemed content to listen and smile and throw in the odd comment. George was the joker, and his wife, Mary, looked on tolerantly when the others humoured him with good-natured laughter. Carrie settled comfortably into the little group, relieved that mealtimes at least would not be an ordeal.

Tom ordered a bottle of wine and they began to study the gold-rimmed menus that had been handed to them by the waiter.

'Sun-ripened avocado fan with sweet grilled red peppers,' Carrie read out to Tom. 'Bit over the top, isn't it?'

He smiled and found one to read to her. 'How about passion fruit and lime chiffon tart?' he said, grinning.

'I used to dance in a chiffon dress once,' she said, and he let out a snort of laughter. The others look up from their menus with puzzled surprise. Carrie straightened her face immediately.

Tom shook his head and continued to chuckle. 'Think I'll settle for steak.'

Jackie asked what had caused their laughter and Tom explained. Then they all started coming up with their own favourites, and were soon in good spirits and the conversation flowed.

The meal went on for several courses, and the food was delicious. Carrie had herb-marinated salmon followed by chocolate parfait, neither of which she had ever eaten before. By the time the meal was finished she was beginning to feel light-headed, not being used to so much drink.

Tom noticed the wobble as she stood up. 'Come on, let's go out on deck for some cool evening air.'

She took the arm he offered and was glad of the support as they made their way out onto a large expanse of wooden deck. The ship was now making steady progress through the various channels and straits towards the open sea. It was almost dusk, the sky streaked with crimson and purple, the white paint-work of the ship taking on a golden glow. There were few people on deck now. Carrie strolled over to the ship's rail to lean on its smooth wooden top and stare out across the water at the splendour of the forested mountains, dark on the distant shores. Music drifted from somewhere on board as several more couples began to appear out on deck.

Tom was standing a little behind her. 'Did I embarrass you at the table when I said how lovely you looked?' he asked, coming a little closer.

She turned to face him and felt herself blushing. 'Yes, but it was nice. There were some amazing dresses there tonight. And I think all the ladies had been to the beauty salon.'

'But you have a natural beauty,' he said. 'You don't need any help.'

He was standing beside her now, and they watched together as the sun finally dipped beneath the horizon, turning the sea into a deep pool of golden ripples.

'I've never really seen anything of the world,' Carrie said.

Tom looked at her. 'Then you must start now. You have a lot of catching up to do.'

She smiled up at him. 'I think work is going to take over when I get home. This is a one-off.'

'What would you like to do now?' he asked. 'I believe there's a show on in the theatre.'

She stifled a yawn. 'I'm done in. I need sleep.'

He nodded. 'Me, too. It's been a long day.'

They watched for a few more moments as gulls circled the ship waiting for scraps from the galley. Then Carrie said good night to Tom and wandered inside and back to her cabin.

But she was restless. All over the ship were people enjoying the various entertainments or just having a quiet drink together in one of the many bars. She sat on her bed in her cabin not knowing quite what to do, feeling somehow left out. She'd only come back to her room because she hadn't wanted to make Tom feel responsible for her; that he had to look after her all the time. But it was still early, and she should be sampling some of the activities on board. It was what she had come for.

There was an art gallery and a library. She could do with a book; she hadn't thought to pack one. And a couple more turns round the promenade deck wouldn't be a bad idea. If she was going to eat all these lovely meals, she needed some exercise.

She grabbed her bag, locked her cabin door, and ventured down the alleyway. Getting in the lift, she pressed for the deck where all the entertainment seemed to take place. Amongst other things there was a ballroom. She'd look in on that first.

As soon as she heard dance music, her feet began to tap. Cautiously she ventured inside. Then she stopped. It was a spectacle of light and colour, decked in drapes of gold and ruby red. Music resonated round the room as couples moved on a dance floor of changing psychedelic colours beneath a crystal ball of cascading starlight.

Rooted to the spot, she took in all this magnificence, hardly daring to go in. The tempo changed to a foxtrot as the band began to play a tune she remembered dancing to with Simon. In her head Carrie was swirling round the floor amongst those dancers, strong arms guiding her. They'd gained a first in that competition, and Simon had picked her up and swung her round and round in his excitement. Nobody could dance like him. He'd been her partner since they were teenagers at the same dancing school. She'd got used to not having Simon in her life, but she would always miss not having him to dance with.

A couple eased past her to get onto the floor, so she moved further into the room to find a corner where she could stand unobserved to watch and day-dream.

A soft-voiced woman crooned into a microphone about this thing called love as more couples got up to move round the floor. Carrie noticed a tall man standing on his own near the entrance who was staring at her. When he caught her eye she quickly looked away. He was probably waiting for his wife. But it made her feel uncomfortable. She didn't want to look at him again, but somehow her eyes were being drawn to where he was standing. Again their eyes met and he began to move towards her. Panic began well up inside her. Then he was standing in front of her, immaculately dressed in black trousers and a crisp white shirt. He had a pleasant face, tanned with a strong chin and sensitive mouth. But it was his dark brown eyes that held her gaze.

2

Love Is in the Air

'May I have the pleasure of this dance?' the tall, handsome man asked, reaching his hand out towards her. His voice was soft and cultured, his smile warm.

Carrie swallowed and tried to control her shaking hands. 'That's very formal,' she said, looking up at him. What on earth had made her say that? She should have accepted his offer graciously. What was wrong with her, that she couldn't even reply to a simple request without making a fool of herself?

His smile took on a hint of humour. 'Is that a fault?'

'No, I'm sorry.'

'So is that a yes or a no?' His voice was gently teasing.

She had to pull herself together. He

had asked her to dance with him. She desperately wanted to dance. She took a deep breath and, putting on a confident smile, placed her hand in his.

As he led her onto the floor, she felt herself stiffen. His closeness both excited and disturbed her. Yet she knew dancing was the one thing she could do with confidence. So why did she feel so nervous?

Once they were amongst the other dancers, he looked down at her with those deep dark eyes and easy smile, took her in his arms and began to move. He didn't hold her close and drift round the floor as all the other couples seemed to be doing, but took a formal ballroom hold and began firmly to lead her into a quickstep. Resting her hand on his broad shoulder, she felt herself relax. The band were playing 'You Make Me Feel So Young'. He was a good dancer and gave a strong lead. The pressure of his hand against her back brought a lightness to Carrie's step as he spun her round to the music, and she did feel young again. She was dancing in the arms of a man who was a good dancer himself, and her feeling of joy was overwhelming.

When the music stopped he gave her a surprised look. 'You dance well.'

She smiled up at him, more relaxed now. 'So do you. I really enjoyed that. Thank you.'

He didn't let her go, but pulled her closer as the band started up again with 'Come On, Get Happy'. They were weaving in and out of the other dancers, who were progressing more slowly, and Carrie's cares of the last few years were dropping away as she remembered how to be happy and have fun.

They continued for several more dances until there was another break in the music. Then he released his hold and looked deep into her eyes. She held his gaze, and something passed between them that had her heart thumping. 'Thank you,' she managed in a breathless voice.

'And thank you, too,' he said, his voice rich and deep. As he led her from the floor, keeping his arm casually round her waist, a warm feeling enveloped her, one she hadn't experienced for a long time.

He escorted her to a table where other people were sitting and pulled a chair out for her. One of the men poured some wine into a glass and put it in front of her, and an elderly lady across the table smiled. 'We were watching you dancing with your husband. You're very good dancers.'

Carrie wasn't going to enlighten them. She smiled secretly to herself. But when she looked to see how her dancing partner had reacted to the comment, he had disappeared. With a sinking heart, she realised he had probably gone back to his wife. As soon as she felt she could leave the others without seeming rude, she excused herself and worked her way through the ship until she was out on deck. The air was cool after the heat of the day, the sea glinting silver in the moonlight, and when she looked up there were a million diamonds sparkling in a black velvet sky.

Hugging her arms round herself as she stood looking over the rail into the still water, she could hear the music resonating in her head. She hadn't felt this lure of romance for a long time, not since Simon. It was a fantasy, she knew. But why shouldn't she indulge once in a while? And here beneath the stars it seemed anything was possible.

Sleep came slowly that night. Such a lot had happened in one day. First she had been terrified and wondered what on earth she had done by coming on this cruise. Then there had been the relief of meeting Tom. But what invaded her dreams was a pair of dark eyes looking deep into hers as strong arms guided her round a magical ballroom beneath a crystal ball of dancing lights to the strains of 'Love Is in the Air'.

When Carrie woke the next morning she shook herself and wondered if it had all been a dream. Had she really met a kind man called Tom, and had she danced with a dark-eyed stranger with a smile that had sparked feelings inside she had almost forgotten existed?

She showered, threw on a pair of shorts and a sun top, and wandered towards the lift in search of breakfast. She was hungry. There were so many places on board to eat. The buffet bar that served continental breakfasts appealed.

Annie was already there tucking into a plate of Danish pastries. Carrie was pleased and relieved to see a friendly face, uncomplicated and safe. She helped herself to some croissants and coffee and went to join her.

'George prefers his eggs and bacon, so he's in the restaurant,' Annie said with a shake of the head. 'He should be the size of a house, but it's me that's got the problem. And he's the skinny one,' she laughed good-naturedly. 'So what did you get up to last night? Didn't take you long to find a man.'

Carrie felt her face flushing and tried to hide it by concentrating on the food on her plate. 'Tom's on his own, too,' she said as nonchalantly as she could. 'We were just keeping each other company.'

Annie chuckled. 'I've heard that one before. Never mind. Go for it, girl. You only live once.'

Carrie shook her head and smiled, happy to let the subject drop.

After breakfast she went back to her cabin to pick up the day's programme of events. There was so much to choose from. But first she wanted to walk her mile round the deck for exercise and then take a dip in the pool.

They were sailing towards the Pacific Ocean before entering the narrow channel that took them up through the glaciers and fjords of Alaska. Carrie stood at the ship's rail for a while, leaning on the smooth wooden top and watching the gentle ripples in the water, its surface sparkling as if the sky had shed all last night's stars onto its surface. Beyond were mountains covered in dense vegetation dropping steeply into the ocean. A sense of peace settled over her as she stared out towards the distant land and listened to the gentle lapping of waves against the ship's side. It was too far away to see any of the wildlife she'd read about, and the sea wasn't offering any either. But there was still the excitement of knowing that at any time it might appear.

People were sitting drinking at the white plastic tables set in front of the deck bar. A light breeze kept the temperature comfortable and the sun shone from a clear blue sky. Carrie went in search of one of the loungers arranged round the lovely curvy pool, all tiled white and blue and full of crystal-clear water. Sculptures of polar bears prowling icy fjords adorned one end. The water looked temptingly cool, but Carrie felt more like relaxing for a while first, so she joined the other sunbathers. She slipped off her sundress, laid her towel on the lounger and adjusted her bikini so that she was sure it was decent. Then she eased herself into a comfortable position and rested her head back on the plastic pillow.

The sun was warm on her face, and soon her mind began to drift until she was dreaming of last night and dancing to that romantic music in a ballroom full of cascading lights. It took her back to the days she'd danced in ballrooms with Simon, dressed in long flowing dresses; how daring she'd felt in her Latin costumes, and how exciting it had been. Last night in the arms of that tall, dark stranger, she'd felt the same spark all over again.

She still had her eyes closed and thought she'd dozed off when a shadow appeared to be blocking out the sun. Her heart began to pound when she opened them and there, standing above her in swimming shorts, all toned muscles and smooth tanned skin, was the man causing her romanticising. Brown eyes peered at her from his ruggedly handsome face, his short brown hair blowing untidily in the breeze. Was she still dreaming?

'So this is where my dancing partner spends her day. Lazing in the sun, I see,' he said with a smile, reassuring her he was real.

'I've already walked a mile round the deck,' Carrie said with a pout.

'Sorry I had to rush off last night. But I'll be there again this evening, if you care for another spin round the floor.'

She lifted herself on one shoulder and shook her head to bring herself back to the present. 'If your wife doesn't mind,' she said, feeling embarrassed but needing to know.

He was unfazed. 'No wife to worry about.'

Relief flooded her. 'Then yes, that would be lovely.'

'It's a rare treat these days to find someone who can dance. Most people just drift round the floor,' he said.

She laughed. 'I know. I have the same problem.'

'I gather your husband doesn't dance, then.'

She shook her head. 'No husband. Here alone.' It was easier just to come out with it and get it over with.

He raised an eyebrow but she didn't elaborate. 'Well, I'm going to take my morning dip.' Then he stopped. 'By the way, I'm Greg. What's your name? If we're going to twirl round the dance floor each evening, we have to know who we're dancing with.'

'I'm Carrie.'

'That's an unusual name these days.'

She shrugged. 'I was named after my gran.'

'It suits you.'

He strode over to the pool edge and lowered himself into the water. Carrie watched as he took off with clean, smooth strokes.

Then she spotted Tom and waved to him.

'How are you this morning?' he asked cheerfully. 'Fully recovered after your early night, I see.'

Something stopped her from telling him she hadn't had such an early night. 'Are you going for a swim?' she said. 'I'm just about ready for a dip. It's quite hot here in the sun.'

'Give me five minutes to get changed and I'll be with you.'

By the time Tom got back, Greg was beside her again, a towel round his shoulders and flip flops on his feet, his bronzed skin glistening with water droplets. Carrie introduced the two men.

'Nice pool,' Tom said.

Greg shrugged. 'Not bad. I've seen worse.'

'Been on a lot of cruises, have you?' Tom enquired.

'You could say that,' Greg said with a wry smile. 'Well, better get going. Things to do.' He gave Carrie a knowing look and headed back along the side of the pool.

*   *   *

As the morning wore on and they sailed further towards the Pacific Ocean, the sky turned grey and a chilly wind blew up. The decks soon emptied, but undaunted, Carrie went back to her cabin and changed into trousers and jacket. She strode round the promenade deck, pausing occasionally to lean on the rail and stare out across the choppy dark water. A heavy mist now concealed the mountain tops in the far distance. As Carrie watched waves breaking against the side of the ship, she could feel the power of the sea seeping into her. Soon the decks were deserted except for a few brave souls in woolly hats and waterproofs, sporting binoculars.

There was someone further down the rail watching her, a man in oilskins, his head obscured by a hood. He noticed Carrie looking at him and came towards her. As he got nearer, she realised it was Greg.

'You're very brave standing here in this weather,' he said, bracing himself against the wind.

She huddled into her jacket. 'You, too.'

'You don't mind rough weather, then?'

'Not at all. I find it exhilarating.'

He stood beside her, looking out across the water.

'I'd love to be up there watching these waves breaking across the bow,' she said, looking up towards the ship's bridge.

He stood back from the rail, rocking slightly. 'Yes, we have some heavy seas ahead and a swell running. Won't last long, though. It'll soon die down.'

'Something of an expert,' she teased.

He gave a short laugh. 'You could say that.'

After a while he turned as if to move on, then paused. 'There's an art auction inside later this afternoon. You might enjoy it.'

'Yes, I saw it in the programme.

Sounds interesting.'

'Well, better get going,' he said and left her standing there as he headed off along the deck. She didn't go in, but watched until he disappeared inside the ship, and then she turned back and continued to stare out across the dark water as the distant mountains began to give way to open ocean. Greg's presence had disturbed her again. What was happening to her? How could he have had such an effect on her in such a short time?

She straightened and shook herself. Where was the harm in it? A bit of light-hearted fantasising might help her to forget Simon. And having a partner to dance with would certainly make the cruise more enjoyable.

Finally she went inside and up to her cabin to change into dry clothes, her mind still on this elusive stranger who kept appearing and then disappearing just as quickly.

★ ★ ★

The ship was buzzing with all sorts of activity when Carrie ventured forth after lunch. Wandering through one of the bars, she was aware of something afoot, then she was offered a glass of champagne. Easing herself through the throng that had gathered, she saw a portly man with a loud voice auctioning paintings. Of course — this was the art auction Greg had been talking about. The auctioneer banged his gavel down, another large canvas sold. The bidding was amazing. There were obviously some seriously rich people on this cruise.

She felt a tap on her shoulder and turned. There he was again, this time dressed casually in slacks and open necked shirt. A frisson of excitement shot through her. He was incredibly handsome.

'Boyfriend deserted you?' he asked.

'If you mean Tom, then I don't know where he is. And he is not my boyfriend.' She tried desperately to sound casual, not to let him see how his sudden appearance had affected her.

He put his hands up in submission. 'Sorry, no offence meant.'

She gave him her sweetest smile. 'None taken. So, what have you been up to this afternoon?'

'Sleeping mostly, I'm afraid.'

'How can you sleep when there's so much to do and see?' she asked, finally managing to control her pulsing heart.

A ghost of a smile touched his lips. 'I've seen most of it. But I enjoy this auction. I'm a bit of an amateur artist on the quiet, and I collect oil paintings. How about you? Are you bidding for anything?'

She laughed. 'No, this is well out of my league. But, never one to refuse a free glass of bubbly, I thought I'd hang around.'

'It's rather crowded in here though, isn't it? The sun's out again and it's quite warm.'

'So you were right in your prediction.'

'I usually am,' he said with a smirk.

'Look, why don't we find somewhere to sit out on deck where we can have a glass in peace?'

Carrie hesitated at first when he indicated that she should follow him, but curiosity won the day. She wanted to find out more about this man who seemed to be trailing her round the ship.

He led her out through one of the doors, along decks, and up and down steps, moving further and further forward on the ship until they came to a small square of wooden deck. It was deserted and had just a round white table and two chairs set up against the ship's rail.

Greg pulled a chair out for her to sit. 'You stay here and I'll get the drinks.'

He disappeared through one of the heavy doors, and Carrie tilted her head towards the sun. The ship was now gliding through still blue water, and a warm glow of happiness consumed her. Drinking wine in the afternoon with an attractive man was the last thing she expected to be doing when she'd boarded the ship.

Within minutes he was back, holding two glasses and a bottle. 'Sorry, couldn't manage champagne, but I think you'll like this.'

She watched as he popped the cork and poured the sparkling wine. 'You know this ship pretty well,' she said.

He handed the glass to her with a smile. 'I like getting away from the crowd occasionally.'

'I don't blame you. It's lovely here. So peaceful. I wonder why nobody else has found it.'

'Could you have found it?'

'No, not really. I just stick to where everyone else is.'

He sat down opposite to her and picked up his glass. 'You should be more adventurous.'

She looked over her glass at him as she sipped the refreshingly cool bubbles. 'This whole thing's a big adventure for me.'

'Are you enjoying it?'

'I am now. I was terrified at first. I thought everyone would think I was odd. I mean, coming on a cruise on my own. But it's been okay.' He was looking at her with that disconcerting focus that made her feel self-conscious, as if everything she said sounded silly and naïve.

'And you found Tom to keep you company,' he said.

'Yes, that helped. How about you?'

He was still regarding her steadily. 'What about me?'

'I expect it's different for a man.'

He inclined his head and considered for a moment, but didn't answer her question.

She sat back, the sun beating down warmly, aware that his eyes were still on her. But it wasn't an unpleasant feeling. If he didn't want to divulge anything about himself, that was up to him. The air was still, the sky was blue, and she was more than happy to sit with him in companionable silence.

'My favourite time of day,' he said

eventually, breaking into her daydream.

She watched as he got up and walked towards the rail, then went to join him. 'I've never been on a ship before,' she said.

Side by side, they stood staring out across the sea. 'And?' he said, turning to her.

All her senses were responding to this man. It really was quite ridiculous, and she must gain control of these feelings before she made a complete fool of herself. 'I love it,' she managed.

'Well, now you know where this deck is, you can come here and have a bit of peace whenever you want to. Just don't let anyone else know about it,' he said, giving her a conspiratorial smile.

She couldn't help wondering if he was alone on this holiday or had come with a friend. But he had an air of confidence she didn't possess, and it made her reluctant to question him further. Better just to keep to small talk. 'It's a completely different world on board a ship, cut off from reality, surrounded by water,' she said. 'All the time you're travelling to unknown places. I'm really looking forward to going ashore.'

They sat again to finish their drinks. After a few more minutes he got up and took her hand to pull her from her seat. His grip was firm. 'Come on then, I'll lead you back to the heaving mob.'

As soon as she was on her feet, he released her hand, and the feeling of disappointment she experienced surprised her.

Once back on the promenade deck, he stopped and looked down at her, and that something special passed between them again. Then he was gone.

Carrie stayed out on deck for a while, looking out towards the horizon across the wide stretch of water, her mood pensive. She'd heard all about love at first sight. Now she wondered if such a thing could be possible. Then she shook herself and turned to go inside.

He was just another passenger being friendly. He'd asked her to dance with him because she could dance well, and he seemed to enjoy her company. Maybe he was lonely too, and glad of someone to chat to. She should be treating his advances in a casual way, be flattered by his attention, and put all ideas of romance out of her head. After this week she would never see him again. She had a busy life waiting for her when she got home.

Falling in love was the last thing she needed. Yet something deep inside her was telling her that this was exactly what was happening.

3

Waiting for Greg

Carrie had never been to a beauty salon before; had never even considered it. A quick trim at the local hairdresser's was enough to keep her curls under some sort of control. But today was different. She was on a cruise. She had leisure time and she felt like indulging herself. Tonight she would dance with Greg again, and she wanted to look her best. A new hairdo would give her the confidence boost she so badly needed. With some trepidation, she walked into the elegant glass-domed reception area of the salon and asked for an appointment.

Luckily they could take her straight away. Sally, a small girl with sleek blonde hair and a friendly face, escorted her to a plush chair in front of a gilded mirror.

Carrie stared at her reflection: pale face, slightly reddened with the sun; fair, curly hair — nothing to show she had just fallen in love with a complete stranger. Again she shook herself and tried to concentrate on what Sally was saying. She had not fallen in love and was never going to again. Love hurt. It had to be avoided at all costs.

Standing behind her and smiling into the mirror above her head, Sally asked what she would like her to do.

Carrie shrugged. 'I really don't know. I'd just like something a bit different. I want to look nice for tonight.'

'You have great hair,' Sally said, undoing the band round Carrie's ponytail and running her fingers through to release the curls. 'It's a lovely warm colour. Why don't I give you a scalp massage, a deep condition-ing treatment to make it shine, and then style it so that it waves more gently from your face instead of the curls?'

'Sounds great,' Carrie said, relieved Sally was making it so easy for her.

As she applied lots of lovely-smelling potions to Carrie's hair and gently massaged her scalp, Sally told her how this was her first trip on a cruise ship, and how she missed her family and often felt lonely, but was determined to settle in and make a go of it.

Carrie was enjoying the experience more than she had expected. Amidst the potted palms and gentle background music, her mind settled and she found herself dreaming about dancing with Greg again that evening. A little flirtation was harmless enough, so long as she kept her head and didn't start reading too much into it. At the end of the week they would go their separate ways, so no harm could come of it. It was just part of her holiday, something to take home and remember.

She loved the way Sally had done her hair, and came out feeling pampered and light-hearted, knowing she would look her very best tonight. Although she was nervous about meeting Greg again, she was excited too.

★ ★ ★

The Harlequin Bar was Carrie's favourite, exotic and colourful, with orange globes of light sending a warm glow over walls hung with rich tapestries, and strange Eastern music quietly playing in the background.

As usual, Tom was there waiting for her. The dress code for this evening was casual, so Carrie wore a short flared dress with a halter neck, its simple line fitting neatly into her small waist. The rich tropical colours of the material made her feel quite heady, a feeling she hadn't experienced since her dancing days. Red strappy sandals completed the look, and with her new hairdo she felt good.

An Oriental bench set against one wall caught Carrie's eye, and she examined it more closely while Tom ordered drinks from the bar. The seat rested on two carved elephants, the back painted with reclining ladies dressed in long robes. Carrie placed herself in the centre and posed with her hands on her lap pretending to look prim, unaware that Tom was watching her.

When he flicked out his camera she felt herself blush. 'I can't resist that one,' Tom said, so she smiled and let him take his photo.

They sat beside each other on a rather upright sofa upholstered in deep green velvet with shiny mahogany arms. The waitress who brought their drinks wore a long skirt and patchwork jacket with dangly earrings that swung as she moved the glasses from a black lacquered tray onto a multicoloured tiled table.

'I haven't seen you all afternoon,' Tom said after he'd given Carrie an appreciative look.

'Not surprising with the size of this ship,' she quipped. Then she told him about the art auction, and they discussed the change in the weather. She didn't tell him about her rendez-vous with Greg. 'So what have you been doing all afternoon?' she asked.

'I went to the wine tasting. Very good, it was.'

'That's why you look so chirpy tonight, then,' she joked, and he raised an eyebrow.

When they'd finished their drinks, Tom got up and shrugged into his jacket. 'Well, I suppose we should go and eat.'

The dinner, as usual, was served with finesse. The food was delicious, and it was nice chatting to the others at the table about their day. Afterward, Carrie and Tom wandered outside to watch the sun sinking towards the horizon in the fading blue of a darkening summer sky. It was quiet now, the air cool and fresh with soft shadows falling across the deck.

'It's nearly ten o'clock and still quite light,' Carrie said.

They were leaning on the rail looking out over the sea. 'We're sailing north. Soon be in the land of the midnight sun. Once we get to Skagway, it'll only be dark for a few hours.'

Carrie straightened up and stretched her arms in the air as if to do a twirl. 'How lovely. I think I shall stay up all night and wait for the sunrise.'

Tom turned towards her. 'You're quite the romantic.'

She quickly composed herself and felt a stab of guilt at thinking about dancing with Greg later. Trying to disguise the excitement in her voice, she said, 'Not really. I'm making the most of this fairytale existence before reality kicks in again.'

'Are you staying for the extra two weeks in Vancouver when we leave the ship?' Tom asked.

'No. I was tempted, but felt it was too much of an extravagance.' She hadn't wanted to spend all her money on this one holiday. 'How about you? Are you staying on?'

'I would have liked to, but unfortunately I only had two weeks of holiday left.'

When Tom said he was retiring for the night to his room to read up on the town of Juneau, their next port of call, Carrie drifted back to her cabin and began to transform herself into the romantic woman she had felt like when she'd been watching the sunset. She couldn't wait to get down to the ballroom and be transported into that fairytale land in Greg's arms as they danced round the floor to dreamy music.

Scanning her wardrobe, she decided on the full-length dress in deep blue that brought out the colour in her eyes. It was off the shoulder, simply cut, and draped her figure perfectly. She'd bought it especially for the cruise but had wondered whether she would have the courage to wear something so lovely. But now that she'd seen how the other ladies dressed up in the evening, she knew it would be perfect. After taking particular care with her makeup, she stood back to view the finished effect in the full-length mirror. With soft waves falling round her face and the glow she felt deep within her, she could hardly believe the image staring back at her was the timid woman who had joined the ship only two days ago. Then she sat on the edge of the bed in nervous anticipation until she judged it was the right time to make her way to the ballroom.

Again she stood in awe as the crystal ball sent rainbow-coloured sparkles over the ceiling and walls. Musicians were playing a romantic piece while a deep baritone voice resonated round the room. Dancers clung together as the floor changed from orange to deep scarlet then brilliant blue.

People were sitting round with drinks and it was impossible to see faces clearly in the dim lighting. But she would know Greg by his stature. And he would be looking out for her, so she edged round the perimeter among the tables, keeping her eye out for him.

* * *

After half an hour scanning the ballroom, Carrie knew he wasn't going to turn up. She bought a drink and looked round for somewhere to sit, not wanting to go back to her room to sit on her own and mope. She had to stay here and try to enjoy the music and watch the dancing. She had to get a grip of herself, not let herself slide into despondency and spoil her holiday for the sake of a man she'd met on board who couldn't even be bothered to turn up when he'd arranged to meet her.

She spotted Annie and George, so went to join them. They could always be relied upon to cheer her up.

'Tom not dancing?' Annie asked.

Carrie shook her head. 'No, he's swotting up on Juneau for tomorrow.'

Annie laughed. 'Not another one. This one here's been at it all day.' She gave George an affectionate look and he frowned.

'I just enjoy watching the dancing,' Carrie said.

'Of course you do, dear. You're a dancer. I remember you telling me. Pity you haven't got anyone to dance with. My George would dance with you if he could dance. I'd love to be able to myself.'

'You could learn whilst you're on board,' Carrie said. 'Brett and Heidi do lessons during the tea dances and they give demonstrations.'

'Now that's an idea,' Annie said, giving George a nudge. 'Yes, I saw it in the programme.' She turned to George. 'We'll go tomorrow.'

George nodded noncommittally, but Carrie knew he'd do anything to please Annie.

'Pity Brett wasn't here tonight,' Annie said. 'He would have danced with you. That's part of his job, you know, to dance with ladies who don't have partners. Must be his night off.'

Carrie sighed. It would have been nice to dance with anyone.

As the evening wore on, George bought them more drinks. Eventually Annie said they were going to bed. 'You don't want to stay down here on your own,' she said to Carrie with concern.

'I'll just finish my drink,' Carrie replied, and Annie gave her a motherly look.

Although she didn't want to admit it to herself, deep down Carrie was still hopeful that Greg might turn up. The band were playing a waltz now, and the singer was crooning 'Are You Lonesome Tonight?'. Carrie's heart tightened and she gulped down the last of her glass of wine.

After sitting on her own for a little while longer and watching as the dancers thinned out, she stood up unsteadily, determined to go. It was well after midnight. She shouldn't have waited for Greg this long. She shouldn't have waited for him at all.

Making her way back to her cabin,

she felt more alone than she could ever remember, and with a heavy heart undressed and crept into bed. Love always hurt. She mustn't let it happen again.

★ ★ ★

Carrie woke early the next morning after a restless night and vowed to steer clear of Greg from now on. She would explore all the ship had to offer and enjoy Tom's company. He was a decent man and had become a good friend in the very short time since they'd met. But that was all, so she had nothing to fear there. Her feelings for Greg were different and could easily get out of hand if she let them.

After a quick shower she pulled a cotton jacket over her sundress and wandered out onto the deck to watch a grey dawn breaking over distant mountains. Ripples on the silver-grey water resonated with her restless heart. She shouldn't be feeling like this. She had to pull herself together. With a determined step, she made her way through the ship in search of breakfast.

* * *

As the ship entered the narrow passage of water cutting into Alaska, the scenery became spectacular. A warm sun was now burning off the mist to show the surface of the sea, smooth as frosted glass. People were flooding onto the decks, all wanting a view of the ribbon-like fjords and snow-capped mountains of Tracy Arm, and then to sit and watch the scenery as the ship cruised slowly towards Juneau, their first port of call.

Carrie stood at the ship's rail to get as close as she could to the huge granite cliffs covered in dense primeval forest rising high above iceberg-dotted water. There was a cry of excitement as someone spotted a large moose standing feeding on an outcrop of rock, its huge antlers rising high in the air. Then everyone was rushing to the other side of the deck. Carrie followed them and stood in awe at the sight of a narrow winding fjord of incomparable scenic beauty, waterfalls tumbling from its glacier-carved domes into blue crystal water.

As soon as they berthed in Juneau, Carrie was down the gangway, not wanting to miss a minute of her time ashore in this strange and beautiful land. Tom had kept her a place on the bus that was to take them to the Mendenhall Glacier, and she gratefully slid in beside him, pushing all thoughts of Greg and her disappointment of last night from her mind.

The old bus rattled and shook them into the town; the dark-skinned driver explaining that he was of the Eagle Tribe and that Juneau was virtually cut off from the rest of Alaska by mountains, the only way in and out of it being by ship or plane.

They got off the bus in a wild, cold place just out of the town and followed

66

their guide to the edge of the great glacier. Carrie stared at the blue-grey mass of ice snaking down a ravine between mountains thick with pines and spruce until eventually merging into a lake of still water glinting coldly in the morning light. She shivered, and Tom put an arm round her shoulder as they stared in silence.

Walking back to the bus stop, the guide pointed to a bald eagle in a tree and talked a bit more about the wildlife of the area. Then there was a stir as they all waited for the bus to take them back into town. Tom followed the direction everyone was looking in. Then he turned, white-faced, to Carrie.

'What is it?' she asked, trying to see what was causing the alarm.

Tom pointed. 'Up that tree. Can you see it?'

She tensed with fear as she spotted a great brown bear. And he was coming down. She gripped Tom's arm and he drew her to him.

'It's okay,' he said. 'The bus is here.'

They scrambled on board and breathed a sigh of relief, then everyone was laughing at their more-than-comfortable encounter with the wildlife they had all been anxious to see.

Back in town they found a bar. Inside it was dark, crowded and noisy, with guns in cases decorating the walls and wagon wheels suspended from the ceiling. Stuffed animals peered out amidst dark wood and heavy furnishings.

Carrie was glad to get outside again onto the wide pavement lined with long, flat buildings painted in light pastel shades. Snow-capped mountains circled the town, their sheer dark slopes set against blue and white sky. A brown and yellow trolley bus trundled along the middle of the road. Otherwise there was little traffic.

They watched the Mount Robert tramway make its way to the summit with its cargo of sightseers, then they looked in the shop windows. Carrie had heard of the famous tanzanite stone on sale everywhere and wondered if she might buy some. But on looking in several jeweller's, she realised it was way beyond anything she could afford.

* * *

The ship sailed late that evening, and Carrie stood out on deck watching as it manoeuvred from its moorings and past another cruise ship moored ahead of her, its great white side dotted with rows of lifeboats, bright orange in the fading light. Beside it, tree-covered slopes, scarred by the remains of an old gold mine, dipped sheer into the sea.

Tom had gone off to watch a film that Carrie didn't fancy. She was reluctant to go into the ballroom again, as she knew she would be looking out to see if Greg was there, and she couldn't face another disappointment. So she stood leaning on the ship's rail, looking out over the water as the sun dipped out of sight into a golden sea. The gentle rhythm of the ship moving through the water was soothing. But however hard she tried, she could not stop herself from wondering where Greg was now, and who he was with. The few people who had been out earlier had disappeared, yet she didn't want to go back to her cabin. She knew she wouldn't sleep. Her mind was too restless.

It was getting quite dark, and she was still standing at the rail watching the water ripple by when she heard footsteps approaching.

'You're up late,' Greg said quietly as he came and stood beside her.

She wanted to be cross with him. She'd vowed she would ignore him from now on. But as she felt the warmth of his closeness, what she wanted more than anything was to stand there with him in the moonlight and just let the happiness of the moment wash over her.

He shifted a little until his arm barely

touched hers, and she felt herself tense. Had he done that intentionally? And if so, what did it mean? She wasn't sure if she should pull away, but the closeness was pleasant, so she stayed still. For a few moments they stood together in silence, absorbing the stillness of the night. Then he turned to go.

'What about my dance?' It was out before she could stop herself.

He paused for a moment and gave an apologetic smile. 'Sorry, not tonight. Maybe tomorrow.'

She turned her gaze back out across the gently eddying water so he wouldn't see the disappointment in her eyes. After a moment she heard his footsteps receding across the deck. Her heart twisted with pain. He'd done it again, and she'd let him. She'd let him make a fool out of her. How desperate her plea must have sounded. Holding back the tears, she quickly made her way back to her room.

★ ★ ★

Early the next morning, the ship tied up alongside the quay in the gold-rush town of Skagway. Determined to put Greg completely out of her mind, Carrie showered and dressed and was down for an early breakfast.

Tom caught up with her as she was going down the gangway. He looked dreadful. 'Carrie, I'm so sorry, but I can't make it today. Must have eaten something that didn't agree with me. I've been up all night.'

'Oh Tom, I'll stay with you. You don't look at all well.'

He shook his head vigorously. 'No, don't think of it. I just need a day to recover. You go off and tell me what I've missed when you come back.'

She was reluctant to leave him, but realised there was probably little she could do, and that he would prefer to be left in peace.

As she followed the others for the short walk into the centre of the town, she was aware of someone trying to catch up with her. She turned just as

Greg drew alongside. He looked happy and relaxed in shorts and an open-necked shirt. She turned away and continued to walk.

'Hey, what's wrong?' he said, taking hold of her arm.

She shrugged him off and continued to walk, keeping her head down so that he wouldn't see how her lip was quivering. How dare he treat her like this? Deep down she knew she was overreacting, and that she should behave indifferently towards him. But her emotions were shooting all over the place, and the only way she could deal with them was by being angry.

He kept pace with her, his tone now more serious. 'Carrie, what's the matter? Is it because of the other night, about not being there for that dance I promised you?'

She said nothing, but could sense him shaking his head and frowning.

'I didn't do it on purpose. I couldn't get away, and last night I just needed some sleep. I'm sorry.'

She tried to outpace him, and after an uncomfortable silence he hung back and let her stride ahead. Determined not to let him spoil her day, she caught up with Annie and George. They wouldn't mind her tagging along with them.

All around them huge mountains reared skyward, enclosing the town within their snowy peaks, the lower slopes richly covered in scrubby green vegetation. When they stopped to look at some ancient locomotive engines parked on rails in an open-air museum, Carrie took a furtive look back to see if Greg was still following. But all she saw was the ship in the distance towering above the town as if sitting in a car park at the end of the road. He'd disappeared again, and again the disappointment was hard to bear.

George was minutely observing a huge black and red engine puffing steam into the chilly air. 'Just look at that. Can't you just see it pulling one of those old trains up through mountain passes into the Yukon, crushing its way through ice and snow? Nothing would stop it. That's got some power.'

Carrie tried to share George's enthusiasm, but all she could think about was Greg. However hard she tried, she kept wondering where he was. If only she could get those searching eyes out of her mind.

'Are you going on the train journey up into the gold rush country?' Annie asked, bringing Carrie back from her reverie.

She shook herself and tried to focus on Annie. 'No, I thought I'd rather look round the town.'

'That's what we decided.' Annie nudged George. 'Come on, Carrie and I are dying for a drink. You've spent enough time ogling those old engines.'

George gave her a despairing look. 'How can you say that? Those old engines have a heart and a soul.'

Annie took his arm and steered him towards the main street, and Carrie followed. Part of her wanted to go off on her own exploring the town. But the encounter with Greg had unnerved her. She couldn't stop thinking about him; how much she'd been looking forward to dancing with him, and how he'd disappointed her last night with his brief appearance. And the way he'd casually spoken to her just now and then disappeared again. Being with Annie and George was comfortable, and it helped to take her mind off him.

Long clapboard buildings in cream and green stood neatly along the wide street against a backdrop of rugged mountains. People strolled along enjoying the sunshine with little traffic to disturb them. A horse-drawn carriage stopped in front of a beautiful old hotel, all yellow and gold with a pagoda tower. The air was fresh and clean, and Carrie felt her spirits begin to lift.

'Used to be a small fishing village,' George said. 'The Alaska gold rush changed all that.' He pushed open the door to a bar and held it for Carrie and

Annie to go inside. It was like a set from an old movie: dark-panelled, low-ceilinged and dimly lit. A few figures, scarcely visible in the gloom, sat round small tables. Behind the bar, a man in checked shirt was polishing glasses and chatting to one of the regulars. Carrie and Annie looked at each other in amusement.

'*Blazing Saddles!*' Annie said.

'Hardly changed since the Klondike gold rush in the 1800s,' George remarked as he stared at the old cracked leather boots, fur hats and stuffed trophy animals on the walls, even real sawdust on the floor.

Again Carrie looked round to see if Greg was there. She wasn't sure whether she wanted him to be there or was relieved he was not. They found a corner away from the bar and sat chatting and drinking. George and Annie were easy company, and Carrie stuck with them for the rest of the afternoon as they strolled round the town and browsed the shops.

Late that afternoon, Greg watched from the deck of the *Flora May* as Carrie walked back along the quay towards the gangway. A shaft of sunlight lit up the curls blowing round her pretty face. She wore short white trousers with white canvas shoes and a pale blue top. A string bag was slung over her shoulder, and large dark glasses hid her beautiful eyes. She didn't seem to bother much with make-up; didn't need it with her delicate skin. Not the usual cruise type. It must have taken a lot of courage to travel alone like that. She was chatting happily to Annie. It was good she'd palled up with that couple. They'd look after her. And Tom seemed a decent guy, too.

He'd walked back to the ship when she'd refused to talk to him, his heart troubled. He'd upset her by not keeping his promise of the dance, and he should have been more chivalrous last night, not walked away and left her standing there. He would have loved to have stayed with her in the moonlight and talked and ended up with her in his arms on the dance floor, but it just hadn't been possible. He knew he'd hurt her, and now she wouldn't even speak to him. She seemed so vulnerable; must have been badly hurt in the past to react like that. Well, he knew all about hurt.

He turned away from the rail. The ship would soon be sailing. He doubted he'd have another chance to see her tonight . . . unless he could think of a way. An idea was beginning to form in his mind. Desperate times needed desperate measures.

4

A Shock for Carrie

Tom seemed fully recovered when Carrie went to his cabin to check on him. 'Slept it off,' he told her.

'Well, I'm glad to hear it, because it's the captain's champagne reception tonight. We don't want to miss that.'

'Not when I've brought my dinner jacket,' Tom laughed.

They met up later in the Piano Bar, an intimate little place in the interior of the ship with deep red furnishings and gentle subdued lighting. A white grand piano stood in one corner, the pianist swaying dramatically as his hands swept over the keys, filling the room with a Beethoven sonata.

They found a couple of comfy sofas to sink into whilst they listened to the music. A waiter in smart white jacket was immediately at their side, and Tom asked for gin and tonics. He knew Carrie's preference now.

Carrie told Tom about her day and had him laughing at George's enthusiasm for the old engines. 'I'd have liked to have seen those.'

'Don't think Annie was too impressed,' Carrie said.

'They seem a happy couple. I was talking to George. They've been married for fifty years. Can you imagine that?'

There was a note of sadness in his voice, but Carrie couldn't help thinking that at least Tom had had a marriage, and known true love. She envied him that.

The waiter placed their drinks on the copper-topped table between them.

'I never drink at home,' Carrie told Tom.

'Well, you're not at home, so it's allowed,' he teased.

They leant back and listened contentedly to the music. Carrie couldn't put a name to the piece the pianist was playing now, but recognised it as one of her favourites.

Others were gathering, all dressed up tonight for this special reception when they would finally meet the captain and his officers. Tom looked smart in his dinner jacket and bow tie, and Carrie felt good in her cream evening gown with the fine straps of tiny seed pearls. She loved the simplicity of the cut and the silky softness of the material. If only she had more opportunities to wear such a dress. Anyway, she was going to enjoy wearing it tonight. She'd even managed to smooth her hair back into gentle waves, the way Sally had styled it, and the sea air and sunshine had finally put some colour into her cheeks. Yes, tonight she felt good, and she was determined to make the most of the occasion.

And, by the way Tom was looking at her, it had been worth the effort. But she couldn't help wishing it was Greg looking at her that way. Then she quickly put the thought from her mind and finished her drink.

Tom looked at his watch. 'Come on then,' he said, standing up and putting out his hand to gently pull her up from her seat. 'Duty calls. Can't keep the captain waiting.'

'Do you know what it's all about?' Carrie asked Tom as they followed the stream of couples making their way towards the restaurant where the reception was to be held.

'I think the officers line up and shake hands with everyone as they go into the restaurant, and then we get a glass of bubbly and that's it. But I've heard the captain's going to dine in the restaurant tonight. Evidently there are some important people on board he wants to entertain.'

'Really? I haven't come across any.'

'Well, we might spot them tonight.'

'So where does he normally eat? I haven't even seen him yet,' Carrie said.

'Oh, I expect they have an officers' dining room somewhere. He won't want to dine with the riffraff every day. Anyway, it won't affect us. We'll still have our usual table.'

They took the lift and, once on the restaurant deck, joined the queue waiting to shake hands with the officers. Mature ladies in long evening dresses with neatly styled hair chatted with their menfolk, who all looked very much at home in tuxedos and bow ties. The whole thing had an air of excitement about it, and Carrie was glad she had Tom beside her, as she knew she would have felt awkward if she'd been on her own.

As they got nearer, Tom eased Carrie ahead of him. She straightened her dress and smoothed her hair, grateful that Sally had done such a good job on it. An older lady behind her was doing the same thing, and they smiled at each other.

'Don't know why we bother,' the lady said. 'I mean he's only doing his job, isn't he?'

'I suppose so. But it all seems very

grand to me,' Carrie said.

The lady hunched her shoulders and her bright eyes twinkled. 'It's what makes these cruises special. Gives us an excuse to dress up. I quite like a bit of glamour occasionally.'

Carrie shook hands with the first officer, a pleasant young man in a smart uniform with lots of gold braid. The next one in line had even more, and he spoke a few words of welcome as he passed her on to the next one. They all looked so handsome in their dark navy uniforms and peaked caps, and Carrie wondered if they would have the same appeal dressed more casually.

As she moved along the line, smiling at each, she began to feel more relaxed. Soon she'd be sitting with Tom and the others, laughing about all this performance and finding out what they'd been doing today.

They were getting towards the end of the queue, beyond which was a large reception area where the tables had been cleared away and white-coated waiters stood with trays of champagne. Carrie felt she'd done enough hand-shaking now and had her eye on one of those glasses of bubbly.

The lady in front of her finally moved on and Carrie stepped forward to take her place. This officer, the last one in the line, must be the captain.

The blood drained from her face and she thought she was going to pass out. He took her hand in both of his, overpoweringly handsome in his uniform with all the gold braid, his tanned face dark against his crisp white shirt, those brown eyes holding her gaze, an amused smile lightening his expression.

She was totally confused. The whole thing seemed surreal. There must be something wrong with her. It couldn't be him. She'd been dancing with him. And he'd stood her up. And then he'd chased after her and she'd refused to speak to him. And now he was holding her hand with those smiling eyes, looking straight into hers. And her heart was pounding in her chest and her knees were in danger of buckling under her.

Eventually she managed to take her hand from his and move away, aware that Tom was saying something to him about being a dark horse and having them all on. Greg answered him, and they continued with a few more words that Carrie didn't take in. Then she was being moved on by Tom towards the reception area.

Like an automaton she took a glass, her hand shaking so much that half the champagne spilt onto the floor. Tom was guiding her into the hub of people already gathered. He was about to say something to Carrie when they found themselves in a group, and Tom was forced into polite conversation. Carrie hung back a little and took another gulp of her drink whilst desperately trying to stop her hands shaking so that she wouldn't make a complete fool of herself.

The talk was lively and Tom entered into the spirit of it, chatting to everyone, glancing at Carrie occasionally with a concerned look. He tried to bring her into the conversation but she could think of nothing to say.

Waiters moved effortlessly through the crowd, topping up glasses. After what seemed an age, the area began to clear as people were shown to their tables. Tom edged Carrie towards one of the waiters, who consulted his seating plan and indicated that she should follow him. Tom was whisked off by another waiter whilst Carrie was being escorted towards the centre of the room.

Finally she found her voice. 'We sit together,' Carrie told the waiter, looking towards Tom.

'We have a special seating plan for tonight. You are one of the captain's guests,' he politely informed her.

Carrie stared at him, then resigned herself to follow. She didn't care where they put her so long as she could reach a seat.

When she saw where he was heading,

she stopped. The waiter stood to one side of the centre table, waiting for her to take her place. It was the seat next to the top one, the one she knew Greg would take.

She shook her head. The waiter looked perplexed. 'Captain Winton has requested you sit here.'

Carrie was beyond arguing and moved to where he was indicating. She stood uncertainly behind the chair and, gripping the back of it, glanced round in a daze.

It was a long table, seating about fifteen people, and slowly it was filling with older couples, all of whom had an air of importance about them. Carrie gathered from the conversation that it was a great honour to be chosen for one of these dinners. There were a few glances her way, but mostly the guests were more interested in each other.

The table was immaculately laid with small gold-edged place cards. Carrie read her name on the one in front of her and it confirmed that she really was meant to be sitting there. Huge gold-edged menus stood in front of each place setting, and Carrie hoped she'd be able to make out what the various dishes were. She'd always had Tom to help her before as they'd laughed at the way they were described. Anyway, her appetite had totally deserted her, and she didn't care what arrived on her plate so long as it wasn't too much.

They were all waiting expectantly now for the captain and officers to come in. The lady opposite her was looking at her with interest. When Carrie caught her eye, the woman gave her a patronising smile.

Carrie could feel her colour rising. 'I really don't know why I've been asked to sit here,' she stuttered, wishing the floor would open and swallow her up.

'Do you think there's been a mistake?' the woman asked in an affected voice.

Carrie swallowed. 'I don't know.'

Everything that was happening was beyond her.

There was a hush in the room as the officers began to take their places at the other tables. Last of all Greg walked into the room and, taking up his position at the head of the table, acknowledged his guests. Carrie tried not to look at him but couldn't help it; he was so incredibly handsome in his uniform. His eyes held hers for just a moment before she averted her gaze, then a waiter pulled the chair out for Carrie to sit and she eased herself onto it with a feeling of relief.

She glanced nervously at the people sitting round the table. They were all elderly couples and, after briefly acknowledging the captain, they began to study their menus, giving serious thought to what they might choose. Greg turned to Carrie, his eyes searching hers. Their mutual attraction crackled in the air between them until she turned away.

'Am I forgiven?' he said in a soft

voice so that only she could hear.

She picked up the menu and pretended to study it. Lobster bisque. She had no idea what that was. She'd never tasted lobster in any form and was quite sure she wouldn't like it. Steak was a safe bet, but that required a lot of chewing. She needed something that would just slip down without her noticing.

'The lamb's good,' Greg said. 'Always very tender. I'd go for that, and the crab cocktail to start.'

She knew he'd been watching her indecision and she nodded gratefully, relieved to see that the others at the table were still busy discussing the menu and not staring at her, wondering who on earth she was.

When the waiter came to take their order, Greg asked for the wine list, and after studying it for a moment was quite specific about the type he wanted. When it arrived he poured a glass for Carrie and then filled his own. Several more bottles were placed on the table, and the others began to read the labels and decide which they would prefer.

'I think you'll like this wine,' Greg said quietly. Carrie knew nothing of wines and was sure that Greg was aware of it.

After sharing some pleasantries with the rest of his guests, he seemed to be waiting for the hubbub of conversation to resume round the table. Then, his voice no more than a whisper, he turned to her. 'Carrie, I'm sorry. I wanted to explain this afternoon, but you weren't in the mood to listen.'

She didn't know what to say to him and didn't want to draw attention, so turned and began a conversation with the man next to her, who seemed happy to oblige. She'd heard him addressed as Professor Beechcroft, but he told her to call him Norman and that his wife, who was sitting on the other side of him, had been an actress. He said they liked cruising because she suffered from asthma and the sea air helped her condition.

Carrie was happy to listen as it gave her a chance to regain some composure. Greg was back in conversation with the loudly spoken woman sitting on the other side of him, the one who had given Carrie that look and who was now trying to impress Greg with all the places she'd been to on previous cruises. Greg was putting on a good show of being interested but Carrie could tell he wasn't. She wondered what he would say if the woman asked him who she was and, despite her inner turmoil, couldn't help smiling to herself.

The meal was delicious. The wine had relaxed her. Greg had been right; the lamb was tender and she had no problem eating it. The others were chatting amongst themselves, trying to impress each other, and Carrie felt at last she was coping with the situation.

While they were choosing desserts from the menu, Greg had the opportunity to speak to her again. 'So what do I have to do?' He raised an enquiring eyebrow.

'Stop playing these silly games,' she said, trying to keep her voice steady. Then she turned to the waiter, who was ready to take her order for dessert.

When she glanced back at Greg, he looked so distraught that she suddenly felt sorry for him. This was obviously his way of trying to put things right between them. But why had he pretended to be a passenger when he could easily have put her in the picture the first night he'd danced with her?

'Can we talk later?' he asked as they drank their coffee. The look he gave her was unnerving, and all she could do was nod.

When the meal was finished, Greg left the restaurant without a word to her, but the light pressure of his hand on her shoulder as he got up told her he would be seeking her out before the night was through.

★ ★ ★

They sailed that evening with a party on the poop deck. After dinner Carrie had hurried back to her room and sat on the end of her bed, trying to make sense of what had happened. Finally she had given up and decided that sitting and brooding was no good, and she might as well go out on deck and join in the merriment.

Now, standing alone watching groups of friends and couples around her laughing and chatting, her courage deserted her. Paper lanterns strung from the masts glowed in the softly fading light. Tom had disappeared straight after dinner and Carrie hadn't seen him since. Greg would be up on the bridge now, navigating the ship out of port, standing tall and handsome in his uniform, taking charge in that confident manner of his. She couldn't spot Annie and George, so looked around for anyone she could talk to. But they all seemed to be in groups, some drinking cocktails from tall frosted glasses, others beginning to dance to the music.

Eventually Carrie went to stand at the rail and stared out with unseeing eyes across the vast expanse of water. Sky and sea took on a warm glow as the sun dipped towards the horizon in a darkening summer sky. A Brazilian group of musicians was playing a rhythmic piece she longed to dance to. The whole atmosphere was full of romance and Carrie felt totally alone.

Then a pair of strong arms encircled her, took the glass from her hand and placed it on the nearest table. Greg turned her to face him and began to guide her in amongst the dancers. As they moved to the rhythm of the music in that small space in front of the musicians, he gathered her close. Smiling eyes met hers but neither spoke; it would have spoiled the magic.

As the sun sank below the horizon and streaked the sky scarlet and gold, Carrie relaxed in Greg's arms, and her loneliness was replaced with a warm glow of happiness, dancing with the man of her dreams in the land of the midnight sun. If it lasted just a minute or an hour, it didn't matter. Here and now was all she cared about. Here and now in the arms of this man.

★ ★ ★

Some time later, most of the partying crowd had dispersed and Carrie and Greg were left together in a quiet corner out on deck. The ship was ploughing steadily ahead, the sea a smooth sheet of dark water reflecting a strip of moonlight and a sprinkle of stardust.

Greg stood beside her at the rail. 'Carrie, I'm sorry I keep upsetting you.'

She looked into his handsome face, shadowy now in the moonlight. 'Why did you do that — make me sit with all those stuffy people I didn't know?'

'I didn't know how else to get you to spend time with me so I could explain. And I wanted to do something nice to make you happy.' He paused. 'I think I failed again.'

He looked so downcast that she wished she hadn't been abrupt with him. 'Why didn't you tell me who you were?' she said more gently.

'I was going to. That's why I followed you this afternoon. But you seemed determined not to listen.'

She looked up at him in the moonlight and her heart melted. 'You could have told me the first night we danced.'

He nodded. 'I know. I wish I had now. But I like to mingle with the passengers sometimes. Most of them don't know who I am until the champagne reception when they meet us all. I just wanted to be me for a while. And I thought it would be just that one dance. I had no idea I was going to feel this way about you.'

She stared at him, unable to believe what she was hearing, and despite her best intentions a surge of excitement shot through her. It was more than just one dance. He had feelings for her, feelings to match her own. And he was searching her eyes for a response. Her heart was thumping. She was speechless, not knowing how to react, what to say. Excitement, fear, confusion — every emotion was surging through her. She turned away, not wanting him to see how much his words had affected her.

Eventually she found her voice and glanced up at him. 'I thought you'd be up on the bridge now.' It was an inadequate response, and from the look he gave her, not the one he was expecting. But she couldn't think what else to say, and she needed to keep her emotions under control; fill the silence before it became too uncomfortable for both of them.

He gave her an amused smile. 'No, I have officers up there who are quite competent. They'll find me if they need me.' He was so mature, so in control. Beside him she felt gauche and unworldly.

He moved away from the rail, turned her to face him, and took both her hands in his. 'And I had more pressing things on my mind.'

She felt herself relax. The awkwardness had passed.

'So where's Tom?' he said.

'I haven't seen him since dinner. We're not together. We only met on board here.'

'I know.'

'How did you know?'

'I checked the passenger list,' he said nonchalantly.

'But how did you know who I was?'

He raised an eyebrow at her tone of voice. 'You told me your name down at the pool. There are no other Carries on board. It was lucky you had such an unusual name.'

She pulled away from him. 'So you snooped on us?'

'Carrie, I simply wanted to know if you were here alone or with someone. If you were with Tom, I wouldn't have pursued you. If you want me to leave you alone, then I will.' He looked deep into her eyes. 'But I'd much rather we went into the ballroom and had that dance.'

'I'd like that too,' she said in a small voice.

* * *

Carrie was still in a dream the next morning as she thought about dancing with Greg in the ballroom into the early hours, how he'd escorted her back to her room, and the look he'd given her as he'd left her at the door. That look had stayed with her until she'd eventually fallen into a deep sleep.

Greg had feelings for her. She didn't know where they would lead; knew in her heart they couldn't lead anywhere. But for now she was content to dream.

This morning they were sailing towards Glacier Bay, where the ship was to hold its position for an hour in order to get close to the glaciers; they'd be able to watch as the enormous ice sheets shed great chunks into the freezing water. Carrie had been looking forward to this part of the cruise since she'd seen pictures in the brochure back home.

First she had to find Tom. She had no idea what he'd thought about the dinner last night; how she'd been whisked off to sit with Greg while he'd been escorted elsewhere. He hadn't appeared at all during the evening or this morning. The thought that he might have been upset by what had happened worried her.

Going along the alleyway leading to Tom's cabin, she heard the sound of somebody sobbing. Following the sound round a corner, she found Sally in a small storeroom looking heartbroken, her face buried in a pile of folded towels.

'Sally, whatever's the matter?' Carrie asked.

The girl turned a blotched face towards her but couldn't speak for the great gulping sobs she was making. Carrie put an arm round her shoulder and made comforting sounds as she stood waiting for her to gain control. Eventually the sobbing subsided and Sally was able to speak.

'She said I wasn't cut out for the job. She's going to recommend that I go home when we get back to Vancouver. She said I wasn't up to it.'

Carrie frowned. 'Who's she?'

'Meryn, my boss. She doesn't like me.' She burst out in a fresh bout of sobbing, and Carrie could only just make out what the problem was.

'It's 'cos I'm always upset. She said it's affecting my work. But I can't help it. I do try. I miss my mum. But I don't want to go home. I love my job and I'll get used to it. But she won't give me a chance. She said I should have got to grips with it by now.'

Carrie hugged her and stroked her back. Slowly the sobbing subsided, and Sally drew away and turned a tear-stained face up to Carrie.

'Sally, I'm so sorry. It doesn't seem fair when you're so good at your job. You put me at my ease the other day. I was quite nervous when I walked into that salon.'

Sally stared at her. 'Were you?'

Carrie smiled. 'Yes, I often am when I'm out of my comfort zone. It happens a lot on this ship with all these well-travelled people.'

'Gosh, I never would have guessed. You seem so confident.'

'Well, I'm not. I just work hard at it.'

'That's what I'm trying to do. But she won't listen. And now I'll be going home in disgrace.'

'It might not come to that.'

Sally burst into another fit of sobbing. Carrie did her best to comfort her and eventually Sally did manage to pull herself together.

'I have to go,' she said. 'We're really busy in the salon today and they're waiting for these towels. I don't want to get into more trouble for being too long.'

Carrie watched her hurry down the alleyway and felt saddened that the lovely, cheerful young girl who had done her hair only days ago had been reduced to this. She decided she should go and see this Meryn and get to the bottom of the problem. There must be some misunderstanding. Sally had probably got the wrong end of the stick.

* * *

After several enquiries, Carrie found Meryn in her office. She was sitting at a computer and looked over her glasses as Carrie went in.

'I wondered if I could have a word with you about Sally, one of your hairdressers. She — '

'Do you have a complaint about her work?' Meryn interrupted.

'No, nothing like that. She did a good job on my hair and was very pleasant.'

'Then what is it you wish to discuss?'

Carrie stiffened. 'I found her in tears the other day — '

'Yes, I'm quite aware of her problems. They are being dealt with,' Meryn said with a toss of her head.

'But that's what I wanted to talk to you about.'

'No need. It's none of your concern. Now if you don't mind, I am rather busy.'

Meryn had already turned back to the screen, and Carrie realised she would get nowhere with this woman. Feeling frustrated and annoyed at her dismissive attitude, she continued on her way to check on Tom, and bumped into Annie and George in the alleyway.

'Come on, dear, we won't see the glaciers calving if we don't get out on deck. You don't want to miss that, do you?' Annie said.

'Have you seen Tom?' Carrie asked Annie, knowing they had rooms near to each other.

'Yes, he came out of his cabin just ahead of us. He'll be up there already.'

Carrie felt easier. At least he wasn't still poorly.

There had been no reason to panic. The ship was still gliding softly towards Glacier Bay with all its magical fjords and inlets. Beneath a cold white sky, the air was crisp and silent, the atmosphere electric with anticipation. It seemed everyone was out on deck and marvelling at the rugged brown mountains dropping sheer into the icy water, their snowcapped peaks reaching back as far as the eye could see. Sparkling green blocks of ice floated on water as smooth as glass as they were carried out towards the open ocean. Eventually the glaciers began to appear and the ship slowed, ready to hold its position in the bay.

People were crowding out on deck with cameras and binoculars. Waiters were serving hot soup, and a party atmosphere prevailed. Carrie mingled with the crowd but was finding it difficult to see as more and more people pushed forward to get a better look. There was a crisp bite to the air and she put her hands round her cup of hot soup to warm them.

'Just look at that!' George exclaimed, standing beside her and staring at the thousand-year-old glacier cliff with its curving river of ice oozing into the blue-green water. 'Grand Pacific Glacier. Twenty one miles of solid ice,' he quoted from the leaflet he was studying.

Carrie huddled into her jacket and looked in awe at the great mass of ice, then jumped as a chunk of it fell from high above into the water with a thunderous roar, sending a shower of droplets into the air.

George laughed. 'It's calving. That's what they call it. All those icebergs floating in the water came off it. Global warming, that's what it is.'

Carrie didn't want the facts. She just wanted to stare at the magnificence and drama, and the stunning beauty of everything around her in its icy stillness. She wished Greg had been there to share it with her, but was consoled by the knowledge that he was in charge of this huge ship, allowing her to enjoy the experience.

As she edged her way forward trying to get a better view, she felt a tap on her shoulder and turned to see her little steward standing behind her, grinning.

'Captain want you up on bridge,' he said.

Carrie stared at him.

'You come this way,' he said, indicating that she should follow him.

Annie gave her a questioning look, then began to grin. 'Go on, get yourself up there, girl. Not everyone gets invited up on the bridge. Make the most of it.'

Carrie frowned uncertainly. When the steward turned, she followed, not knowing what else she could do without upsetting him. He led her through some alleyways and up in the lift to the bridge deck, from time to time looking back to make sure she was still with him and giving her a toothy grin of encouragement.

5

Too Close for Comfort

Greg was standing, feet apart, scanning the horizon through the thick glass window that spanned the whole width of the bridge. Carrie waited uncertainly at the entrance as the steward went up to him. She could hear Greg's deep masculine voice giving orders from time to time. The bridge was enormous, with walls of instruments flashing lights and churning out information. Two officers were bent over a huge map spread out on a chart table beneath an overhead light. Another stood checking a reading on a big brass domed instrument.

All the officers were busy and, when one of them looked up and saw her, it took all her willpower to stop herself from turning tail and running back to the safety of the deck. Then he smiled at her reassuringly and she relaxed a little.

After speaking with the steward, Greg turned and saw where she was standing and beckoned her to come over. She cautiously eased her way forward to stand beside him, then turned and gave him a questioning look.

He backed off. 'I haven't upset you again, have I?'

When he rested his arm lightly on her back to point out the various glaciers, she felt a warm glow of happiness. And when another great chunk of ice fell off the glacier with a crashing roar, she gasped and he gently squeezed her shoulder.

'Impressive, isn't it?'

They watched for a few minutes, then he spoke quietly. 'You told me you'd like to watch from the bridge of the ship. So now you are.'

'I didn't know who I was talking to then.'

Again that amused smile. 'I'm still the same person.'

He dropped his hand from her back, and as their fingers touched momentarily a tingle shot up Carrie's arm. Their eyes met, and the look that passed between them had her heart thumping. She pulled her gaze from his and looked around the bridge, trying to distract herself from the intensity of what she was feeling.

'I'd no idea it would be like this,' she said, trying to keep her voice light.

He'd moved slightly apart from her now, but still his look was searching. 'Are you disappointed? Not what you thought the bridge of a ship ought to be like?'

'I didn't expect to see all this equipment.'

This time he threw back his head and really laughed. 'Times change. Everything is done with computers these days.'

'You don't usually let passengers up here, do you?'

'Only important ones,' he said.

'Well, you can hardly put me in that

category. Won't they wonder who I am, the other officers?'

There was a touch of mischief in his voice when he answered her. 'They'll wonder. But I won't enlighten them. Keep them guessing.'

She shook her head and smiled, then turned to admire the view again.

'You have the most beautiful eyes,' he said, taking her by surprise.

One of the officers who'd come up to Greg with some information gave her an amused look, and she felt her colour rising and looked away.

'Sorry,' he whispered when they were alone again. 'I've done it again, haven't I?'

She looked up at him and shook her head slowly. How could she be cross with him when he was looking at her like that?

Nobody was taking much notice now. They all had their jobs to do to hold the ship in position so that the passengers could enjoy the spectacle. When Greg gave orders for them to sail he stayed beside her, but was now more alert and watchful as the ship manoeuvred out of the bay. From time to time he wandered over to take some reading or speak to one of the other officers, then came back to Carrie to point out various landmarks: the other great glaciers and, in the distance, various mountain ranges. She soon lost her nervousness and became absorbed in what Greg was explaining as the ship made its way through the narrow channels and out into a wider stretch of water.

'This land is so big and wild,' Carrie said, in awe.

'Yes, it's a beautiful place. Mostly been turned over to national parks now, which is good. It'll preserve the wildness of it.'

'I don't think I could live here, though. What do the people do?'

'Hunting, fishing, gold mining. They make good use of their natural resources.'

Greg wandered over to the far side of

the bridge and spoke to a younger officer who was looking with a puzzled expression at one of the instruments. Carrie continued to stare out through the glass. The sky was a clear blue, and all she could see in every direction were soaring mountains and floating icebergs in water as smooth as glass.

She was so absorbed in her surroundings that she jumped when Greg came up behind her. He leant over and placed a pair of binoculars to her eyes, and as he did so his hand gently rested on her shoulder. He bent so that his face was alongside hers, and pointed. 'Can you see the moose feeding near the edge of the water?'

She found the huge cow-like animal and gave a shriek of delight. When Greg's fingers touched the back of her neck an involuntary shiver rippled down her spine, and she gripped the binoculars tightly to stop her hands shaking. Then he slowly began to caress the skin at the top of her neck with his thumb and she couldn't stop a silent

116

gasp escaping her lips. He'd felt that gasp and slowly moved his hand down her spine so that all her senses were now responding to his touch. And he knew it. She'd lost focus on the moose and all she could see was brown forested mountainside, her head swimming and her body a lump of quivering jelly.

Greg took the binoculars from her, strode over to the table and began to study the big chart. Eventually he called her over and pointed out the ship's course, taking care not to get too close this time. She tried to concentrate and keep her voice steady as she made sensible comments. But her mind was in turmoil. When she said she'd go down, Greg gave her a knowing look that did nothing to steady her. He seemed to be a little shaken too.

Once amongst the other passengers again, Carrie had a strange feeling of not being really there, and so set off, her feet pounding the deck. She had to keep moving to try to get her equilibrium back.

They were in open water again now, and the sky had turned grey. A mist hung over the sea and a slight turbulence began to disturb the surface. Staring over the ship's side, Carrie saw the churning water, which seemed in tune with her troubled mind. She couldn't afford to have these feelings for Greg. Falling in love was something to avoid. She wasn't about to let another man break her heart.

Yet later when the sun came out and she'd installed herself on a sun lounger on the lido deck, she began to feel a bubble of pleasure that Greg had remembered how she'd said she would like to go on the bridge. It showed he'd been thinking about her.

She must have dozed off, as the next thing she was aware of was her name being called softly. Looking up, she saw Greg staring down at her. She pushed herself up into a sitting position.

'All right for some of us,' he laughed. 'How did you enjoy the glacier?'

'Impressive,' she said. 'You're full of surprises.'

He perched on the end of her sun lounger. 'You did want to come up on the bridge, didn't you?'

'Yes, of course. It was amazing seeing those chunks of ice falling into the sea. And the whole scene from up there was so impressive. I wouldn't have been able to see half as much from the lower deck with all those people around me. Thank you.'

'Are you coming for a swim?' he asked.

'Not just now. I might later.'

He got up to go but she stopped him. 'Greg, I wanted to ask you something.'

'Go ahead,' he said, his face clouding momentarily.

'It's a bit difficult. I don't want to get anyone into trouble.'

'But . . . ?' he said with a questioning look.

'I found one of the young hairdressers in tears earlier. Sally. I don't know if you know her.'

He shook his head. 'Not my department.'

She frowned. 'I thought the whole ship was your responsibility.'

His jaw tensed as he regarded her and she knew he wasn't pleased. 'Carrie, I can't do everything on a ship this size. That's why we have a cruise director. Meryn will sort it out.'

He was about to turn to go then, when he saw the look on her face, and hesitated. 'Right, what's the problem?'

Carrie picked up her book and opened it. 'Go and have your swim,' she said dismissively.

He stood looking down at her. 'Carrie, I asked you a question.'

She gave him a hard look. 'Sally is distraught. Meryn's told her she's going to send her home in Vancouver because she's homesick and not up to the job. She did a very professional job on my hair. She has a lovely manner. She's young and she needs to be given a chance to settle.' She turned back to her book with studied indifference.

He nodded, then walked over to the pool and dived into the water.

★ ★ ★

Carrie was taking her usual walk round the deck later in the afternoon when Greg appeared up one of the ladders just ahead of her. She ignored him, but he waited, then fell in step beside her.

'I had words with Meryn,' he said. 'Sally is not going home, and will be given the support she needs. I've sent a report to head office about Meryn's attitude. Your name was not mentioned.' He picked up speed and left her standing staring after him.

Carrie didn't know whether to laugh or cry. He'd done what she wanted him to do. But his manner indicated he didn't approve of being told his job. And she knew she really shouldn't have interfered, but had felt so sorry for Sally. Anyway, the outcome for the girl was good, so it had been worth making Greg angry.

At five every afternoon, tea dances were held in the Starlight Room. Though smaller than the main ballroom, it had a good-sized dance floor. Carrie had looked in yesterday on her way back to her cabin to change for the evening but hadn't quite had the courage to go in. It had seemed so full of people and chatter. Brett and Heidi, the professional dancers, were already giving the lesson, and she felt she couldn't interrupt.

Today she was determined to venture inside. Standing at the entrance trying to pluck up courage, she took a deep breath. The atmosphere was gently romantic as people sat listening or danced to organ music played by a thin, straight-backed man with sleek hair and wearing a pale blue tailcoat. The whole room was bathed in blue light from a star-studded dome high above, from which ivory folds of gossamer silk draped down to walls of deep purple.

George and Annie were sitting at one of the tables, which gave Carrie the courage she needed to go in. After chatting for a while, they sat back listening to the music and watching those who were already on the dance floor. Everyone was waiting for Heidi and Brett to appear for the demonstrations and to teach some new steps for them to try out.

'No sign of any lessons today,' Annie said disappointedly. 'Heidi and Brett haven't shown up.'

Carrie frowned. 'They should have it underway by now. According to the programme, the session started half an hour ago.'

Annie sighed. 'Just our luck. I was really looking forward to it.'

'Look, there's Brett,' Carrie said as she saw him walk into the room.

'And about time,' Annie said. 'He's very good-looking, isn't he?'

Carrie had seen Brett dancing with passengers on board during the sailing parties and had hoped he might ask her to dance. But he hadn't noticed her, always gravitating towards the ladies who joked with him and drew his attention. But she could see what Annie meant. He was good-looking, well-built and about her height, with white-blond hair that dipped across his forehead in a quiff. Every inch a dancer.

'Heidi's a very good dancer, too,' Annie said.

But there was no sign of Heidi. Brett seemed a little flustered and went to speak to the organist. The music stopped and the floor soon cleared. Brett stood on the small raised platform and announced that Heidi was ill and couldn't take the session with him today. There was a groan of disappointment. He said he would try to teach the steps they'd planned but unfortunately there would be no demonstration, as he didn't have a partner to dance with. There were frowns and mumbles all round. It was something everyone who attended these sessions looked forward to, watching the professionals dancing the steps they wished they could do themselves.

George seemed relieved, but Annie's face dropped. Brett was talking to a group that had gathered round him, then he ran his fingers through his hair and frowned.

Annie turned to Carrie. 'You're a dancer, aren't you? You could do the demonstration with Brett.' She didn't wait for Carrie's response but shot straight up to Brett, tapped his arm and pointed back to Carrie. At first Brett looked puzzled, then he shrugged and they exchanged a few words. Several eyes turned towards Carrie, and then Annie came rushing back, her face beaming.

'He wants you to have a go if you're willing. I told him you would be. I mean, you love to dance, don't you?'

Carrie couldn't help smiling at Annie's enthusiasm. She was reluctant to get up and put herself forward in this way. But if it meant all these eager people could learn to dance, she would do her best.

She got up and made her way warily

towards Brett. He put out an arm to welcome her, a look of relief on his face, and she was soon facing an audience of expectant dancers. Brett explained what he wanted her to do. It seemed fairly routine, and she knew she would have no difficulty with the waltz turn he suggested.

'I'd like them to see us dance it first,' he told her. 'Are you okay with that?'

'Yes, of course.'

The organist began to play a waltz and the lighting dimmed. Brett took hold of Carrie's hand and led her to the centre of the floor. She relaxed as he took up a ballroom hold, feeling that familiar excitement at the start of a dance.

They began to move round the floor doing basic waltz steps, and in the corner they did the turn Brett wanted to teach. Carrie easily slid into the rhythm and felt comfortable with Brett's firm lead. Then he began to lead her into more advanced steps, and she realised he had forgotten about the lesson as he spun her round the floor. She was soon lost in the rhythm and music. It was a long time since she had danced like this. Brett's poise, strong lead and perfect timing, even on the most intricate steps, was pure magic.

*   *   *

Greg had only come down to the Starlight Room because he wanted to see Carrie and, knowing how much she loved to dance, had guessed this was where he might find her at this time of day. He'd been abrupt with her out on deck when he'd told her about dealing with Meryn and he wanted to make amends.

Standing at the entrance, he scanned the room. It was full as usual. These sessions always attracted a good crowd. It was surprising how many people wanted to learn to dance, given the chance. He'd had lessons years ago, long before he'd come to sea. And it had paid off. He enjoyed going down to the ballroom in the evenings for an hour or two.

He was surprised to see Carrie and Brett dancing on their own with everyone watching. As he stood there, his brow furrowed. She danced so beautifully, almost like a professional. Then the thought struck him: maybe she *was* a professional dancer. He'd been surprised at how easily she followed him when they danced together. He really knew very little about her.

The tempo changed as the organist began to play 'Fly Me to the Moon'. Brett began to sweep Carrie round the floor, swaying and turning with the music. They made a good pair. Brett certainly had charisma, and Carrie looked so pretty in her short sundress. Her feet in the dainty sandals hardly seeming to touch the ground. She was a different woman from the rather timid one who always seemed to look out of place on this ship.

Brett twirled her to a close with a flourish, and she bobbed a curtsy as he held her at arm's length. He must have remembered he was supposed to be giving a lesson. But those watching hadn't had enough. They cheered and clapped and insisted on more.

Brett obviously preferred to dance rather than teach, and as the organist went into jive mode, he and Carrie really got into their stride. She was so quick on her feet, never missing a step or turn, her control perfect. Her curls were piled high on her head, the way she wore her hair when she was sunbathing, golden tendrils trailing down her neck. Greg preferred it that way over the sophisticated look she tried to assume in the evening. She was a different woman, so confident, so vibrant. And she could certainly dance.

His heart was full. He wanted her more than any other woman he had ever known. From that first dance the night they sailed from Vancouver, he'd been in love with her. The way she'd stood at the edge of the ballroom all alone and looking so lost . . . there was something so delicate about her. He'd behaved badly towards her, he knew. He didn't seem able to stop himself from doing it again and again. It was his only protection against getting too close, too involved. And he couldn't let that happen.

She seemed vulnerable, and he didn't want to hurt her. The only way was to keep his distance. But seeing her dance like that, so happy and full of life, made it difficult. He couldn't stand watching any longer. He had never felt like this before, and it was tearing him apart knowing how much he wanted her and that he could never have her. Slowly he walked from the room.

★ ★ ★

Carrie didn't see Tom until that evening when she met him in the Silverwood Bar before dinner. She loved this bar with its red bucket chairs arranged round brass-topped tables. Large glass windows allowed a perfect view across the sea to distant shores as the ship slid by in the gentle light of an evening sky. A soft-voiced woman was singing love songs into a microphone. Carrie tried not to listen to the words. 'Beware My Foolish Heart' wasn't something she wanted to be reminded of.

Tom didn't look quite his normal self. 'How are you?' she asked.

'Better,' he said. 'I enjoyed Glacier Bay. I tried to find you but there was such a crowd.'

'I did come looking for you, but Annie told me you were already out on deck.' She paused. 'Sorry about dinner last night. I didn't want us to be separated, but it appeared I had no choice.'

He gave her a resigned smile. 'That's okay. How did you enjoy dining with the captain?'

Carrie blushed. 'It was awkward.'

'Never mind. Back to normal tonight,' Tom said, not quite managing his usual warm smile. But things *weren't* back to normal, and Carrie wondered if they ever would be again.

He noticed her hesitation. 'Hey, cheer up. We have the celebrated baked Alaska parade tonight.'

They were still deciding where to sit when there was a shriek from somewhere near one of the windows. An excited group was gathered and pointing out to sea.

'Whales on the port bow,' someone shouted, and more people rushed to try to see them.

Tom steered Carrie towards the large picture window they were looking through and she squealed with delight. In the distance she could see several of the huge creatures playing in the water. First a sleek black head would appear, followed by the tail fin as a multi-ton humpback jumped for joy high in the air, spraying sparkling droplets over the golden water.

As they went in to dinner, Tom commented on how nice Carrie looked. She was getting used to his compliments and knew they were well-intentioned. And she did feel good this evening in the close-fitting rose-coloured dress she had chosen to wear. 'I miss not having the opportunity to dress up since I stopped dancing,' she said.

The others were already sitting at the table, and the men stood as Tom pulled out the chair for Carrie to sit. Then he took his place beside her.

'You certainly have the opportunity to dress up here,' he said as they picked up the menu. 'And you do it so well.'

'Mum and I used to spend hours sticking sequins on my dance dresses,' she told him.

Jackie picked up on this, and Carrie felt herself flush scarlet. But it seemed they were all interested in her dancing career, and she found herself the centre of attention throughout the meal, regaling them with her various dancing pursuits. She didn't mention Simon. It would have spoiled the evening.

'I could get used to feeding like this,' she said as they tucked into a deliciously spicy chicken dish. They all agreed the food was very good.

When they sat back to wait for desserts, there was a stir in the restaurant as loud music issued forth. Waiters in smart blue and red uniforms came marching in, banging gongs and singing patriotic songs. Chefs in tall white hats, each carrying a baked Alaska high above their heads, joined the line as it progressed round the restaurant, the diners now on their feet cheering and clapping.

'My mum used to make that dessert,' Carrie told Tom once they'd been served.

'I don't even know what it is,' he admitted, taking a mouthful. 'But it tastes good.'

Carrie laughed. 'It's ice cream baked in a meringue case. You have to bake it in a very hot oven so the meringue browns but the ice cream stays frozen.' As she took her first mouthful, Carrie thought about her mum and fell silent for a while.

'Memories?' Tom said, giving her a sad smile.

She looked up at him. 'Yes, but good ones.'

Tom suggested they go see a film after dinner, but Carrie didn't fancy it, so he went off on his own while she went out on deck for a breath of fresh air and to watch the sunset. Glancing up at the bridge, she imagined Greg in his uniform, his far-seeing eyes ever watchful. The ship was bound for Ketchikan now, sailing south again through calm waters, away from the land of the midnight sun; yet the sky was still a blaze of colour. Standing at the rail watching the mountains slip by, Carrie found the gentle ripple of the water soothing.

She had never been so aware of the beauty of sunsets before coming on this holiday. As she stood at the ship's rail staring at sea and sky in their constantly changing colours, she thought about how she seemed to be changing too. Troubling thoughts kept intruding, forcing her to reassess her life. Was that a good thing? She wasn't sure.

She'd happily agreed to work with Julia and thought it was what she wanted. Yet after dancing with Brett that afternoon, she knew she wanted more. Was it just the romance of this holiday away from her humdrum life at home that was disturbing her? Or was it something much deeper that had taken hold of her? Something that had nothing to do with dancing.

She knew in her heart it was all to do with Greg. Getting into this state over him was dangerous. Love was dangerous. She had thought she had found it with Simon, but it hadn't lasted. Love was wonderful for a while, but then it tore you apart. It had taken her a whole year to get over Simon. And even now it hurt to think how he had deserted her when she had needed him most.

No, she had to keep herself grounded. At the end of the week all this would be a memory. She began to pace the deck, determined to bury all these strange unsettling feelings. But despite her best intentions, when Greg appeared on deck her spirits lifted and her mind cleared.

He fell in step beside her. 'Not going to the show? It's a really good one tonight.'

'No, Tom wanted to see a film and I didn't fancy it,' she said lightly.

He cleared his throat. 'I'm sorry if I was a bit abrupt this afternoon.'

She shrugged. 'It's okay. I shouldn't have interfered. But thank you for sorting it out.'

He stopped and turned to look at her. 'I should be thanking you for bringing it to my attention. Sally seems a nice girl. Meryn can be very abrasive at times. I often wonder if she's right for the job.'

'I expect she has a lot on her plate looking after all the crew,' Carrie said as they stood facing each other.

'Yes, but it's what she's employed to do.'

'I hope Sally makes it. She does seem very determined.'

'She will.'

He wandered over to the ship's rail and she followed him. 'I just love these long balmy evenings when it hardly seems to get dark,' she murmured.

'The land of the midnight sun. Yes, it's quite magical,' Greg said, staring out towards the distant mountains, dark now against a scarlet-streaked sky.

'Tom told me that up in north Alaska the sun never sets in midsummer.'

'That's right. And in midwinter it doesn't get above the horizon. Children play out in the moonlight.'

Carrie sighed. 'How wonderful.'

Greg gave her a tender look and held her gaze until she turned away. 'What had you planned on doing this evening?' he asked.

She looked up. 'I wasn't planning on doing anything.'

'Come on, then — I know you'll enjoy this show. Lots of dancing and singing. I've got a few hours off duty, so I'll come in with you.'

6

Difficult Decisions

Carrie had been in many theatres during her dancing career, but this one was beyond anything she could have imagined: seats in plush blue velvet, and cream decor. The stage curtains were a deep blue with lots of gold twirls and tassels.

Greg found them seats near the back with a good view of the stage. As soon as they sat down the lights dimmed, music filled the theatre, and the curtain rose to reveal a stage bathed in brilliant white light. Leggy girls in killer heels, scantily dressed and with plumes rising high from their heads, sashayed onto the stage.

Carrie felt her spirits swell with happiness. In her mind she was up there with those dancers, remembering shows she'd been in, and the thrill of it all. How she would love to be up there now.

The lighting faded to a warm pink, and the music became softly classical as ballet dancers floated on in a froth of pale pink tulle. Then Carrie was watching girls in blue top hats and fishnet tights performing a lively routine with men in black striped suits, an extravaganza of music and dance and colour.

The stage cleared, and a woman in a long shimmering dress walked up to the microphone and began to sing a beautiful love song: 'What next, my love, now that you've left me?' A little shard of pain shot through Carrie. It was something she didn't want to think about.

As the singer stood alone, bathed in glorious golden light, Greg's hand reached across and covered hers. His touch resonated through her body, and when she didn't pull away he took hold of it. Their eyes locked and, at that moment, in the light from the stage, something passed between them that had Carrie's heart beating out of control.

There was an explosion of music and again the stage was full of dancers, this time beneath a dazzling canopy of sparkling orange and white light. The show continued non-stop with constantly changing scenes, each one more spectacular than the last. Carrie's face was aching from smiling in delight. She sensed Greg looking at her, but she couldn't take her eyes from the show, so wriggled her hand further into his and he squeezed it gently.

When it seemed it could get no more dazzling, silver fountains of light began to shoot up through the dancers, changing through all the rainbow colours in time to thumping vibrating music. Carrie's head was spinning. When the music reached its crescendo, the whole stage was a vista of dazzling light, and Carrie realised she was gripping Greg's hand as if she would never let it go. The audience erupted, and as Greg took his hand from hers they joined in the rapturous applause.

When they emerged from the theatre, he guided her to a quiet spot out on deck. As they stood side by side in the moonlight watching the water rippling beneath them, Greg put an arm round Carrie's shoulder, and she felt she had never been happier.

'That was amazing. Thank you so much for taking me,' she said, looking up at him.

His expression changed to one of amused surprise. 'I gather you enjoyed it. You were gripping my hand so tight I think I have nail marks in my palm.'

She felt her colour rising, and his smile had her heart thumping again.

He drew her closer to him. 'I'm not complaining,' he said, his tone pensive.

After a while he turned towards her. 'I saw you dancing this afternoon with Brett.'

She frowned.

'You dance beautifully. I had no idea.'

'It's what I do,' she said.

'You mean you're a professional dancer?' He raised an eyebrow.

She nodded.

'Why didn't you tell me?'

'You never asked.'

He shook his head and laughed. 'It never occurred to me. But I can see it now. The way you move. The way you look. It all fits.'

Then before she could look even more uncomfortable, he enfolded her in his arms and hugged her close.

That night she fell asleep, dreaming of Greg and the feel of his hand covering hers, and his arms around her in the moonlight with just the gentle ripple of the sea beneath them.

★ ★ ★

They berthed in Ketchikan the next day just ahead of the *New Orleans Paddle Steamer*, and the sound of a jazz band playing on board had Carrie dancing down the gangway. She knew that what had happened last night wasn't real and couldn't lead to anything. Yet she hugged it to herself and took pleasure from it. What was the harm, so long as she kept reminding herself it was just a holiday romance?

'Land of the totem poles,' Tom informed her, breaking into her thoughts as they made their way into the town. She tried to compose her face from the inane grin she'd been wearing all morning.

Tom began to explain how totem poles were part of the First Nations culture and that each one told a story. He had pictures of them in his book. Carrie tried hard to concentrate but her mind was elsewhere.

'Sorry, am I being a bore? I'm interested in these things and I tend to think everyone else will be,' Tom said, giving her a sheepish look.

A feeling of guilt pulled her up sharply. 'No, not at all. I wish I'd looked it up. It just didn't occur to me. All I'd wanted was to get away from the house and all its sad memories.'

Tom put his book in his pocket so he could give her his full attention, which made her feel worse, thinking she had hurt his feelings.

After they'd visited the display of totem poles with their colourful carvings of fierce staring faces and strange crouching figures, they went into the town and got a map from the tourist office. Tom suggested it would be interesting to take a route round the outskirts so that they could see how the ordinary people lived. Carrie was happy to go along with this, feeling that in some measure it made up for her lack of interest in the totem poles.

Ambling slowly along, they admired the old cedar houses built into the mountain, while others were on stilts round a lake, with wooden walkways linking them.

Tom stopped and turned to Carrie. 'Can I see you when we get back home?'

Carrie had had a feeling this was

coming, but the suddenness of his words took her by surprise and she felt herself tense. 'May be difficult. We live in different parts of the country.'

His face clouded and she felt a stab of remorse knowing she had not handled it well.

'It's not so far. I feel we're friends now. It would be a shame not to keep in touch,' he said, seemingly unaware of her discomfort.

'Exchange photos and things,' she said lightly, knowing it wasn't what he wanted. But she was glad it was out in the open and she hoped he'd accept it.

'Well, we can do that over the internet. But it's not the same as seeing you. I could come over one day.'

She averted her gaze. This was going to be more difficult than she'd expected, but it was necessary to make her position clear. 'I'm going to be working full-time at the dancing school when I get home. I don't think I'll have much spare time for a while.'

When she saw the sad resignation in

his eyes and the slight droop of his shoulders, her heart twisted with pain. The truth had finally registered, but it wouldn't have been right to give him false hopes. She thought too much of Tom to do that.

He nodded and they continued their walk in awkward silence. When they stopped to study the map again, Tom turned to meet Carrie's eyes, and he gave her a wistful smile. 'It's good to have plans,' he said. 'I'll be straight back to work, too.'

Carrie gave him a regretful smile, knowing he was trying to put their relationship back on a footing she was comfortable with.

Once back in the town amongst the touristy things, their mood lightened. A zigzagging broadwalk on pilings above water took them to Creek Street, notorious for its houses of disrepute when the gold rush was at its height.

A buxom woman in bonnet and long skirt stood outside one of the bars trying to seduce the men inside, knowing all they would see was a museum commemorating its lusty past. Touristy shops now replaced the old sporting houses, but the place still held the spirit of the gold rush days a century ago.

The fish market was bustling and smelly. Then they came across a lumber show and after that watched a blacksmith working at his furnace. Tom had regained his good humour and they enjoyed the rest of the afternoon together.

★ ★ ★

Back on board, Carrie was making her way up to her cabin when she bumped into Sally. It was a different Sally from the one who had been sobbing her heart out the day before.

'You're looking more cheerful today,' Carrie said.

'I feel much better now. I'm sorry about the other day. I don't know what came over me.'

'We all have bad days. Have you sorted it with Meryl? I gather you're not on your way home from Vancouver.'

'No, that's what I was coming to tell you. I'm doing the next cruise.' Then she lowered her voice. 'The captain came looking for me. He was really kind. He asked me what the problem was and he really seemed to care. I think he might have had a word with Meryl, because she's been ever so nice to me.'

Carrie gave her a hug. 'I'm so pleased for you. You're a lovely girl and a talented hairdresser.'

Carrie felt a warm glow as she walked towards the lift, then frowned as she came up to her cabin. Stuck onto her door was a note. It was sealed and had obviously been put there by the steward. Quickly going inside, she tore it open and read the contents.

It was hand-written and simply said: *Dine with me tonight. Meet me on our special deck at eight.*

It wasn't signed. It didn't need to

be. She knew it was from Greg. She stood staring at it, excitement coursing through her. She wanted with all her heart to respond, to be there to meet him, to be alone with him for a few precious hours. But she'd arranged to meet Tom in the Oyster Bar at seven, and that was what she intended to do. She wasn't going to hurt him again.

* * *

Tom was waiting for her, his manner more serious than usual. He stood while she took the seat opposite him. The waiter was immediately at their side, smart in his starched white jacket.

Carrie had tried a few cocktails during the voyage but still preferred her gin and tonic before dinner. But tonight she fancied a change. Greg's note had made her feel light-hearted. Although she was unable to accept his invitation, there was something pleasurable about being pursued by an attractive man, though a little nagging voice in her head was telling her to be cautious. But she was with Tom now, nice safe territory, so she could relax. Picking up the drinks menu, she looked down the list.

'Think I'll go for something different tonight,' she announced.

Tom raised an eyebrow. 'Not your usual gin and tonic then?'

'No, I feel like living dangerously,' she quipped.

'Well, then, what's it going to be?'

The waiter hovered, tray in hand, smiling politely.

'I might try this one,' she said, pointing it out on the menu to Tom but not daring to say it out loud. Tom let out a guffaw and Carrie was relieved to see he was back to his normal cheerful self. The waiter took the order without comment.

'You're a dark horse,' Tom said. 'Whoever would have thought?'

Carrie gave him one of her prim looks, then couldn't help her mouth twitching into a cheeky smile.

'I hear you're dining with the captain again tonight,' he said.

Her smile disappeared. 'Tom, what's going on?'

He shrugged. 'He came to see me when we got back and told me he'd asked you. I think he wanted to clear it with me.'

Carrie was furious. 'He had no business going behind my back like that. And I am not dining with him. I am dining with you as usual.'

Tom shook his head. 'Carrie, I know the score. Look, you go and enjoy yourself.'

'No,' she said firmly.

He shook his head and smiled at her. 'He's going to be disappointed.'

'Well, that's his bad luck. He had no business discussing it with you as if I didn't have any say in the matter.'

Tom leaned forward. 'Okay, don't get on your high horse. He obviously fancies you. Just because he's the captain of the ship doesn't mean he's immune to your charm.'

She shook her head and smiled. Tom could always lighten her mood.

The waiter put the cocktails in front of them. Tom stared at the drink, then looked up at Carrie, his face serious again. 'You know how I feel about you,' he said. 'I made it pretty clear this afternoon. But I'm not stupid. I can see that you don't feel the same. Let's be friends. You go off and spend time with Greg. I can tell you want to.'

She looked straight at him. 'Tom, I do not want to have dinner with Greg. I want us to spend the evening together. Is that clear?'

Tom shook his head and his expression lightened. 'Very clear.'

★ ★ ★

Later that evening, Carrie went into the ballroom to watch and listen to the music. Brett was dancing with one of the ladies Carrie had seen pushing her husband round in a wheelchair. When

153

the music changed, he came over to Carrie and asked if she would like to dance. Helping out at the tea dance had paid off; he now knew she was on her own and liked to dance. She accepted gracefully and he put a hand to her back to lead her onto the floor. A deep baritone voice was crooning songs of love as she floated round in his arms. It felt so wonderful to be dancing again with Brett. He was courteous and friendly and a superb dancer. They did a quickstep followed by a lovely rumba. Finally Carrie felt she had taken up too much of his time.

'That was lovely,' she said as they walked from the floor.

'It was a pleasure,' he said, still holding her hand. 'I enjoy dancing with you. It can get tedious at times doing basic steps.'

'I know what you mean. I feel the same when I'm giving lessons.'

'You teach, then?' he said.

She explained about Julia's dance school, how she'd been helping out since her mum had died, and how she was going to run the school with her when she got home. 'We've got a show to put on when I get back, so that'll liven things up a bit.' Brett listened with interest and, when they got to the side of the room, he led her to one of the tables.

'Will you have a drink with me?' he asked.

'If you can spare the time. I know you're in great demand.'

'I am allowed a break,' he said, smiling.

Once she was seated, he went off to the bar and came back with two glasses of wine. Sitting opposite her, he began to question her further about her dancing experience.

'I took lessons in everything: tap, ballet, street dance. I spent most of my teenage years taking dancing exams and rehearsing for shows,' she told him.

She sighed and shrugged her shoulders. He gave her a questioning look, waiting for her to continue. She was hesitant. 'We had such plans, my boyfriend and I.'

'And?'

She swallowed. 'When I watched the show last night, I wanted so much to be on that stage again.'

Brett leaned forward, his eyes bright. 'Why don't you come on board then and dance with me?'

She gave him a shocked look. 'I don't think Heidi would like that.'

Brett shrugged. 'We're not a couple, you know. We're just dance partners.'

'I still don't think she'd be too happy if I took her job.'

He grimaced. 'Truth is, we're not getting on very well. She seems unhappy and she keeps having off days when she won't dance at all. It's not good.'

Carrie didn't know what to say. She'd seen Heidi dancing with Brett at the tea dance a couple of days ago. She was good, but she held herself very stiffly and there seemed to be no joy in her dancing. With her long blonde hair, she would have been pretty if she hadn't looked so miserable.

'I'm wondering if she's thinking of packing it in,' Brett was saying. 'If she left this trip, would you consider it?'

Carrie shook her head and frowned. 'I think you're getting a bit ahead of yourself here.'

Brett sighed. 'You might be right.' He was thoughtful. 'But you were brilliant yesterday at the tea dance. The way you just stepped in. And you enjoyed it. It showed.'

'But there's more to it than that. I haven't been on stage for years.'

He shrugged. 'I don't think you'd have a problem there. I can tell by the way you dance. But it's really for the tea dances. Everyone loved you yesterday, the way you helped them with the steps after our demo. Then there's the sequence dance sessions when we need to teach new routines. And the late-night disco dancers like a challenge too.'

'Yes, I've looked in on some of those

sessions. But I haven't seen Heidi there.'

'Heidi is hardly ever there. But she should be, that's the problem. She always makes some excuse. And partnering the passengers in the evenings is important too,' he continued. 'She hates doing that. I know you'd be so good.'

She gave him a wistful smile. 'I did it all once. It seems so long ago now.'

Brett sighed. 'Well, it can't carry on like this. It's not good for the ship. Heidi really isn't pulling her weight, and I get all the stick. When I try to talk to her she snaps at me and then bursts into tears. I really don't know what to do. We're supposed to be in the show tomorrow night. I just hope she's up for it when the time comes. It's part of the finale, and it won't go down well if she pulls out.'

'Do you have a routine worked out?' Carrie asked.

'Yes, it's all sorted but we still need to rehearse.' He gave her a pleading look.

'Think about it, please.'

Carry sympathised but slowly shook her head.

'Ah, well, back into the fray.' He stood up and mingled back into the dancers, looking to see if he was needed anywhere.

Carrie sat for a while finishing her drink. Then she saw something that lightened her heart. Sally was dancing. She looked more closely in the dim light and recognised one of the young chefs. They had their arms wrapped round each other and were looking into each other's eyes as they slowly moved to the music, oblivious to all around them. Carrie felt a warm glow followed by a deep feeling of envy, watching young love developing before her eyes and knowing it was always going to pass her by. She felt a sudden sadness that she no longer had anyone special in her life. Finding such a person seemed so hard — someone you loved and who loved you back. But she was happy for Sally. The girl wouldn't be feeling so homesick now.

★ ★ ★

Carrie couldn't sleep for thinking about what Brett had said. A great vision kept opening up in her mind of dancing with him and possibly even getting on that wonderful stage. She tried to dismiss it from her mind. This cruise was really unsettling her. A part of her wanted it to go on forever, yet she felt the sooner she could get home and back to reality the better. She had a life waiting for her. This was fantasy. It could only lead to heartache.

Anyway, Brett had been speaking out of turn. Heidi probably wasn't about to vacate her job. And even if she did, the company would have someone else lined up to take over, someone who was much more suitable for the job than Carrie was. And Julia was expecting her back in a few days. They had a show to put on. Her brother was coming to the airport to meet her and take her home.

She tried to go to sleep but it was useless. Her head was full of music and romance, and Brett dancing with her, and Greg with his arm around her beneath the stars.

7

Challenges for Carrie

It was the last day of the cruise and Carrie was in a sombre mood. The morning began with sunshine, but as they entered the Pacific Ocean a wind got up and it turned cooler. She walked round the deck three times, her usual exercise, all the time thinking about Greg and her conversation with Brett the night before.

She had lunch with Tom and spent time chatting to Annie and George. It was while she was beginning to pack for disembarking the following morning that there was a knock at her door. Sally stood there looking decidedly unhappy. She perched on the end of Carrie's bed and seemed about to burst into tears.

'Whatever's the matter?' Carrie asked.

Sally swallowed. 'It's Rob.'

'What about him? Is that the chef you were dancing with last night?'

'Yes, we've only just got together and he's really nice,' Sally said, trying bravely to hold back the tears.

'So what's the problem?'

Sally's face crumpled. 'He's going home on leave when we dock in Vancouver. And I'm staying here on the ship.'

'Oh, Sally, I'm sorry. You looked so happy dancing together.'

Sally nodded and it took a while before she was able to speak. 'We really like each other. I've never had a proper boyfriend before. And now I've found Rob and we won't be together after today.'

'But what happens at the end of his leave? Won't he come back on this ship?'

'He doesn't know. They could send him on another ship. Then I'll never see him again.' Sally burst into tears and Carrie put an arm round her shoulder.

Eventually she stopped sobbing and got up. 'Sorry, Carrie. I didn't mean to cry all over you again. I just came to say goodbye in case I don't see you tomorrow. I'll be okay now. It's something we have to live with, isn't it, when we choose this life. But Rob says we will get together again somehow. He's really determined about that.'

Carrie was almost in tears herself. Sally was being so grown up and strong, and here she was herself, almost twice her age and not coping half as well. She watched her amble off. Sally had the right attitude. She'd get on. And Carrie hoped Rob would be true to his word.

She stuffed her clothes into the case, leaving out just what she would need for tonight. It was still early afternoon, so she wandered through the shopping aisles and bought gifts for her niece and nephew, hoping it would summon up some enthusiasm for seeing them again. But her heart was heavy. Tomorrow she would leave the ship.

She wouldn't see Greg again. She probably wouldn't see Tom after they landed in London. In such a short time she felt she had become part of this community. Annie and George. Sally. They were friends now. She had never anticipated any of this when she'd booked the holiday. It seemed as if these last few days had changed everything. And now she had to go back and try to settle into a life that suddenly held no excitement for her. She'd be going home to a lonely house, missing Tom's friendship, and dreaming of Greg, dancing with Brett, this ship, and all the emotions that went with it.

Gripping her bag of gifts tightly, she went out onto the deck and threw herself into the nearest deckchair. This was ridiculous. It wasn't like her at all. If Sally could deal with her predicament, so could she. She had a loving family and a loyal friend in Julia. They would soon build the dancing school up and have a thriving business, and she would be doing what she had been trained to do.

It was this cruise that had unsettled her. She should never have come on it. She should have stayed at home and got on with her life instead of gallivanting round the world. She'd go and find Tom. He always managed to cheer her up.

With a determined step, she made her way to the library, a small quiet room lined with shelves of books and furnished with heavy oak tables equipped with Anglepoise lamps, all polished wood and shining brass. Carrie found it oppressive, but Tom seemed to enjoy its peaceful ambience and often spent the afternoon there reading.

Instead of Tom, Carrie found Heidi all on her own, slumped on a low wooden seat and staring out of a small window. Carrie went and perched on the seat beside her. 'Are you all right?'

Heidi turned red-rimmed eyes on her. 'No, I'm not.'

Carrie waited to see if she wanted to talk.

Heidi regarded her sourly. 'You think you can take over, don't you? I know Brett would rather dance with you.'

Carrie straightened. 'What's all this about?'

'Oh, don't give me that. I've seen the two of you. Thick as thieves, you are.' She gave a dismissive noise and turned to stare out of the window again.

'Heidi, I helped out when you were ill, that's all. I'm sorry if it upset you.'

'I bet you are,' Heidi said, still with her head turned away.

Carrie stood up and, after staring at the back of Heidi's head for a moment, decided there was little point in trying to talk to her in her present mood. The verbal attack had left her reeling.

Eventually she turned and left. But it unsettled her. Had she behaved badly stepping into Heidi's shoes that day at the tea dance? Had Brett said something about her possibly taking Heidi's place? If so, she could understand the woman's anger.

Tom was in the Seaview Lounge, the big one that stretched the width of the ship and gave panoramic views through its huge expanses of glass windows. He was sitting on one of the big leather sofas that looked out towards the bow of the ship and beyond. Carrie collapsed on the seat beside him. He put his book down and frowned at her.

'Okay, what's up?'

She stared straight ahead through the window but said nothing.

'It's Greg, isn't it?'

Tears were threatening. She mustn't give way to them. She must keep her focus straight ahead through the glass and let the passing scenery calm her.

'No, it's everything,' she said eventually, forcing herself to look at him.

His cool blue eyes were studying her keenly. 'Carrie, what are you going to do? Have you told Greg how you feel?'

'No, of course not.'

'You should.'

'Tom, he doesn't have those feelings

for me. It's just a bit of fun to him.'

'I think it's more than that.'

She stood up and confronted him, trying to push away the pain with a show of anger. 'Tom, I'm having a bad day. I've had Sally crying on my shoulder again. And I've just been accused by Heidi of trying to oust her from her job. I just need cheering up a bit.'

People round about were beginning to take an interest in this exchange, so Carrie slumped down on the ledge beneath the window opposite Tom. 'Can we talk about something else?' she almost whispered.

Tom leaned forward. 'Yes. We can talk about what you're going to do when you get home,' he said in a quiet but determined voice.

'Fine. I'm going to run a dance school with my best friend. I'm going to get on with my life.' She was trying hard to keep her voice steady.

He leaned back. 'You don't sound too excited about it.'

'Well, I'm not going to mope around over someone who fancies a bit of a flirtation with me to break up the monotony of his job on board here. He's probably got someone at home waiting for him.'

'But you said he didn't have a wife.'

'That doesn't mean he's fancy-free, does it? And he never divulges much.'

'I think you're misjudging him.'

Carrie sighed. 'Tom, there's no point in talking about it. He lives in Vancouver and spends most of his life on board a ship. I live in a Cotswold village and have a family and a job waiting for me. Our worlds are miles apart.'

'They needn't be.'

Carrie felt real anger rising. She stood up and faced him again, oblivious now to the stir she was causing. 'Stop it, Tom!' she shouted. Then she turned and left him frowning after her.

★　★　★

It was to be their last evening on board before docking in Vancouver and disembarking. Then there would be two nights in a hotel with time to explore the city before boarding the plane home.

Carrie ambled out onto the deck. Somehow she could think more clearly out there. It was almost deserted; most people would be packing and getting ready for their last evening on board. The thin mist that had covered the tops of the mountains earlier had been burned off by the sun; the sky was a cloudless azure blue, the sea reflecting a darker shade as rays of sunlight danced on the ripples, making them sparkle. Carrie watched the land slipping by, and the movement of the ship gliding through the water calmed her.

So much had happened over the past week to turn her world upside down, and her emotions were raw. She would miss Tom. It had been good having him by her side all week, someone to laugh with and sometimes get angry with, but also someone who understood her the way he did. She'd never experienced this sort of friendship with a man before. She had few friends back home and no social life at all. There had never been time for it after her mum had become ill. Before that, her life had been tied up with dancing competitions, rehearsing and working out new routines with Simon.

As she contemplated her lonely life at home, she wondered if she was turning down her last chance of happiness with someone she could trust and respect. Tom had made it clear he would like them to continue their friendship, and she sensed he would have liked it to progress further. Could she be happy with Tom? He was a lovely man. Yet there was something missing, something that she felt with Greg. But could a relationship based on romantic love be sound, or was it safer to have companionship with someone you could trust? Carrie didn't think she could settle for that. Round and round her mind went as she stared out over the side of the ship gliding through the clear, calm water.

There were still a couple of hours before she was to meet Tom for their pre-dinner drinks, and she needed something to settle this turmoil inside her. As she made her way back inside, she passed the health spa. That was what she needed, something to soothe her mind and relax her for her last evening on board. She'd see if they could fit her in. After today there would be no time for such luxuries. It would be home and then work.

They had a slot and could take her straight away. A young woman with a soft, calm voice and pleasant manner suggested a head and shoulders massage. It sounded just what she needed.

Quiet music played in the background. A large glass bowl with scented candles floating amidst lotus flowers gave out an aura of calm. As Carrie lay on the warm, soft towels whilst strong hands pummelled her back and eased the tight muscles in her neck, her mind drifted, and gradually she felt herself relax. This whole cruise had been more of an adventure than she'd expected, with so many emotions stirred up. Soon life would get real again. Tonight she would enjoy herself with Annie and George and Tom and try not to think about anything else.

As she came out of the health spa she bumped into Brett rushing along the deck. He stopped when he saw her, a harassed look on his face. 'Carrie, I've been looking for you,' he said breathlessly.

'What's the matter?'

'It's Heidi.'

Carrie groaned inwardly.

'Carrie, you've got to help me.'

She backed off. 'No, Brett. You have to solve this one yourself. I've already had a confrontation with Heidi and I do not want another one.'

'No, there won't be any trouble from Heidi. She's packed her bags and is ready to get off as soon as the gangway's down tomorrow.'

'So what do you want me to do? I'm not going to try to persuade her to stay.'

'I don't want you to do that. I want you to dance with me in the show tonight.'

Carrie stood open-mouthed, staring at him. 'You must be joking.'

'I'm not joking. Meryl's in a state over it all. She's had a go at me. Now she's telling me if we don't get our act together tonight we'll both be leaving the ship tomorrow.'

Carrie shook her head and sighed. 'Brett, what you're asking is impossible. Anyway, you have a whole team of dancers. What does it matter if one is missing?'

'It matters because Heidi is the only one who can ballroom dance. The finale is set in Vienna. It's a tradition on this ship. We always end the final show with this spectacular. I need you to do a Viennese waltz with me. One dance. That's all. It'll spoil the whole scene if we miss it out. All I need is someone who can dance with me.'

Carrie shook her head. 'I can't do it, Brett.'

A look of defeat came over his face. His body slumped, then he turned to go.

'Okay, okay, I'll give it a go. Show me what you want me to do and I'll see if I can pick it up.'

The change in his demeanour was all the reward Carrie could have wished for, and despite her misgivings a spark of excitement shot through her. Greg was forgotten. Her mind was buzzing. She'd done this a thousand times before. She could do it again.

Brett was already hurrying her along the deck to the Starlight Room, which was empty. He sorted the music and Carrie stood waiting for him to show her what he wanted her to do. There would be lots of dancing throughout the show, then the finale would involve the two of them sweeping onto the stage for that one dance. The lighting and costumes would be dramatic, but there was nothing difficult about the dance. Carrie soon felt confident she could do what Brett wanted.

After half an hour they had it perfected. All she had to do was follow his lead. Part of her was terrified at the thought of being on that stage in front of all those discerning eyes, yet a little voice deep inside was telling her that she wanted to do it. This would be a once in a lifetime experience that she would take home and treasure.

'What on earth am I going to wear?' Again panic rose.

Brett was eager to placate her. 'There's a whole room full of dresses left over from other shows. Go and see what will fit you.'

Carrie found the stage wardrobe, a small room with dresses and costumes of every description hanging on rails. There were huge boxes overflowing with bits of lace and feather boas and strange masks. Frothy dresses were bundled onto a shelf, and ball gowns hung from rails round the room. She began to sift through the dresses, but they were all the wrong size or hopelessly unsuited to a Viennese waltz. Maybe she should just wear one of her own dresses, though they weren't nearly elaborate enough for the stage. A feeling of despair settled on her. She needed to feel confident if she was to carry this off. And wearing a dress she wasn't comfortable in wouldn't help. Why on earth had she agreed to do this? But she had, and she wasn't in the habit of letting people down. She firmly believed that the show must go on. And she'd promised Brett.

Finally she managed to find a sequinned dress in pale blue. It was past its best with some of the sequins missing, but it would probably look all right on stage. It didn't quite fit, but if she could borrow a needle and cotton and put a couple of tucks in it round the waist it might look passable. It was the best she could find and it would have to do.

There was a long gap between now

and the evening show. First dinner, then the farewell party out on deck. Brett would be there and she might get the chance to dance with him, even though it would be amidst a crowd of other dancers. Just to get the feel of his style would be helpful and settle her nerves. After that she would go backstage and change for the show.

★ ★ ★

Carrie was so nervous she could hardly eat anything at dinner. She'd told Tom about Brett persuading her to dance in the show but had sworn him to secrecy. She didn't want it talked about at the dinner table. Tom had been encouraging and told her he'd be sure to go and watch her perform.

The farewell party on the poop deck was now underway as the ship sailed on towards Vancouver and the end of the cruise, with flags flying, fairy lights glittering, and waiters with silver trays handing out cocktails in tall glasses. The musicians were in full swing. Everyone was in a party mood, out on deck watching the beautiful sunset. The small area for dancing was quickly filling with couples wanting a romantic evening to end their holiday. Carrie stood on the edge of it all, waiting and hoping that Brett would appear.

★ ★ ★

Greg had had a tiring day on the bridge. They'd hit some fog, and then a wind had come up as they reached the open sea. Finally he had managed to get down for a break and ambled onto the poop deck to see how the party was going. Usually he kept away from these things, but something had drawn him there tonight. He'd tried to ignore it but couldn't. He needed to see Carrie. She'd be there with Tom. But that didn't matter, so long as he could look at her and be near her for a few last moments. Although he'd known her for such a short time, being with her felt more right than anything he had ever experienced or could dream of. Yet he knew in his heart it could never lead to anything more.

It was so crowded that he feared it would be impossible to find her. He picked up a drink from the deck bar, not caring much what it was. He just needed something to relax him. Standing there in his uniform, he felt conspicuous, but he hadn't had the energy to change. And anyway, he was off to bed for a few hours now before they needed him again for berthing in Vancouver in the morning.

But his heart was heavy. He'd never let a woman get to him in this way before. Greg's few relationships had been short-lived. He thought about home and Renée. Women couldn't cope with men who spent most of their lives away on a ship.

He mingled with the crowd. The music wasn't helping. It was slow and romantic, the sort that really made you want to hold the woman of your dreams close. The sky was streaked scarlet, and he stared at it as he so often did. The sea was calm now, a deep velvety pewter, with only the bow waves of the ship breaking the surface.

He looked towards the dance floor. There were couples in each other's arms. Happy couples. But he couldn't see Carrie among them. Brett was there dressed flamboyantly in a tropical shirt for the sailing part, doing his bit partnering ladies onto the dance floor in front of the musicians. He was a conscientious employee, always on the job, dancing with anyone who was sitting alone or whose partner didn't dance. He was trying to steer a large lady round the floor and was finding it almost impossible. But he was smiling at her good-humouredly. Then the music stopped and he escorted her back to her husband. The lady smiled appreciatively at Brett, who then walked to the other side of the deck.

Greg's heart twisted painfully as he saw him guide Carrie into the dancing.

She looked radiant in a simple emerald dress that skimmed her slender figure. It was low-cut at the back, showing her pale creamy skin. Her hair was piled on top of her head in a mass of tight curls, accentuating her fine features and natural poise, with small tendrils escaping down the nape of her lovely neck.

Could that really be the same woman who had looked so nervous at the dinner table amongst all those pompous guests only a few days ago? The woman who had so hesitantly crept onto the bridge in Glacier Bay, fearful that the other officers would wonder why she was there?

Greg couldn't take his eyes off her. Brett had her in his arms and they began to move round the small area of deck in front of the musicians. They were playing 'Unforgettable', a Nat King Cole song Greg had always loved. Carrie *was* unforgettable. He knew that as long as he lived, he would never forget her.

They were dancing close and Greg stiffened. He wanted to go up there and tap Brett on the shoulder and take hold of her himself, but his legs were anchored to the deck. He continued to watch as the music changed to something slow and romantic. Yes, it was the theme from 'Love Story'. A soft-voiced woman was singing into the microphone: 'Where do I begin?' The words drifted through Greg's mind.

Brett had taken his hand from round Carrie's waist and was now reaching out to her. She moved towards him, her arms moving as her body swivelled and turned, so elegant and poised. Then they began to do the most sensual dance Greg had ever witnessed, her hips moving in a seductive way in that silky dress that showed off her figure so well.

Other dancers on the floor began to notice and fell away one by one until the floor was clear as they stood aside to watch Brett and Carrie. Greg could hardly contain himself. It was a rumba, the dance of love.

He was aching with desire for her. She moved so sensually, hips gently swaying, legs perfectly controlled, her head high. She was a different person when she was dancing, so confident, so poised, her movements so fluid.

Greg knew Brett was a superb dancer, but he had never seen him dance like this before. Certainly not with Heidi. Had Brett fallen under Carrie's spell too? Greg could hardly bear to watch them, and yet he couldn't tear himself away. He supposed you could only dance that way with somebody you were in love with. How could a man not desire her? She was so lovely.

Greg clenched his fists. He couldn't watch any more. He'd felt moved when he'd watched Carrie dancing with Brett before, but this was something else. The mask she hid behind was gone. He saw the real Carrie, the one who was so consumed by music and movement that she wasn't aware of anything else — not the people watching, not what they would think of her, just the dance. If only he could take her to him and make her feel like that always; take away the hurt and the fear she had of life.

The lady standing beside him sighed and linked her husband's arm. Everyone was silent and watching. Then, as the dance drew them together, Carrie looked into Brett's eyes. It was the look of love. She was looking into Brett's eyes with that look Greg would have given anything for. He couldn't stand it any longer. With a great force of will, he turned and walked away.

8

A Sad Goodbye

When the dance ended there was a round of applause. Brett led Carrie from the floor and over to the side of the ship, where they stood and watched as the dancing resumed.

He turned to Carrie. 'You dance so beautifully. You're so responsive. I feel I can lead you into any routine and you follow.'

She smiled up at him. 'You give a good strong lead. It would be difficult *not* to follow.'

He shook his head. 'Heidi doesn't think so. She's always complaining that I change the routines and that she never knows where she is with me.'

Carrie shrugged. 'Simon used to do that. I got used to just following whatever he did. I hope it works tonight. I'm really nervous about it.'

His smile was reassuring. 'Trust me, you'll be just fine.'

'Are you sure Heidi's okay with me dancing in her place?'

Brett gave a snort. 'She's point-blank refused to dance tonight. Says she's not well.'

'And do you believe her?'

He sighed. 'I don't know what to believe. But I can see she's in no fit state to go on that stage tonight.' Then he glanced back at the dancers. 'Ah, well, better get back to it. I'll have them complaining that I'm not doing my job.'

Carrie watched him go up to an elderly lady standing on her own and ask her to dance. She beamed up at him as he took her hand. Carrie smiled. He was a nice man. He didn't deserve all this unpleasantness, and she was glad she was helping him out.

She picked up another cocktail from the table where they were laid out and wandered towards the ship's rail, where she could watch the sun sink low towards the sea.

She still didn't feel comfortable about taking Heidi's place in the show. What if Brett had got it all wrong? Suddenly she knew what she had to do. She had to go and see for herself. She'd find Heidi and talk to her.

As she walked towards the door leading into the accommodation, Carrie saw her huddled on the edge of a lounger in a far corner of the deck and hesitated. She would have preferred to have this conversation in private, but there might not be another chance. She had to do it now.

Heidi looked up, her expression bitter. 'Enjoyed that, did you? Everyone watching.'

'I enjoyed dancing with Brett, yes.'

'And the show tonight, I've been informed.'

Carrie shook her head. 'Brett said you were ill and he asked if I'd help. If you feel up to it then I'd much rather you did it. I'm not keen at all.'

'Do I look like I'm going to do it?' Heidi snapped.

'You don't look very well. What's wrong? Can I help?'

Heidi gave a harsh laugh. 'Get me sober, then you might be in with a chance.'

'I think we could do that. You've got an hour or so. Let's get you some strong coffee.'

Heidi shook her head and spoke slowly and carefully in a determined effort not to slur her words. 'Carrie, I am leaving this ship tomorrow. I am packed and ready to go. And I have danced my last dance with Brett. The floor is all yours.' Then her face began to crumple.

Carrie was at a loss as to what to do and instinctively sat beside her and put an arm round her shoulders. 'Do you want to talk?'

Heidi didn't resist but shook her head slowly. 'Take no notice of me. I'm just bitter.'

Carrie could see a faint glitter of

tears as Heidi turned to face her and struggled to continue. 'I'm in love with him. But he's made it very clear he's not interested. It's very difficult to dance with someone under those circumstances. I pick fights with him all the time just to shield myself from the hurt.'

Carrie could feel her pain. 'I'm so sorry.'

Heidi tried to stand but her legs gave way and she slumped down again. 'Nothing you can do. Talking won't change anything. Anyway, I've told the company I want a transfer from this ship next voyage. We can't go on like this.'

'I know. Dancing brings you together in a very special way. That must be hard,' Carrie said.

'It happens all the time on these cruise ships. I'm thinking of giving it up altogether, getting a proper job and having a normal life,' Heidi said without looking up.

Carrie felt her heart clench. What

was normal? Here she was, wishing she could stay on this ship and be with Greg and dance every day with Brett. Yet all Heidi wanted was out.

They looked at each other, an empathy building between them. Then Heidi managed to stagger to her feet with Carrie's help.

Carrie gave her a concerned look. 'Will you be all right? Can I get you anything?'

Heidi turned to her. 'You can come with me to my cabin. I have something for you.'

Carrie frowned but followed Heidi's unsteady progress along the alleyway until they came to her cabin. She opened the door and walked in, indicating that Carrie should follow.

Carrie stood in the small room while Heidi pulled a curtain across a rail. Then she stood back unsteadily and pointed. Inside, hanging in the otherwise empty space, was the most exquisite dress Carrie had ever seen. 'Nice, isn't it?' Heidi said.

'It's beautiful,' Carrie whispered.

Heidi turned to her. 'Take it. It should fit you.'

Carrie stared at her.

'Go on, take it. If you're doing this show tonight you might as well look the part.'

Carrie shook her head violently. 'No, I couldn't. I found a dress in the stage wardrobe.'

Heidi gave out a raucous laugh. 'I've seen that lot of tat.'

'There's certainly nothing to compare with this.'

'Then take it, girl. I'm offering it to you. It's no good to me now. Take it. Just shove it in a bag and give it back to me in the morning.'

Carrie still stared at the dress. Then she turned again to Heidi. 'Thank you.'

Heidi pulled the dress off the hanger and slung it over Carrie's arm. 'Go now. And don't let me down. I know you can do it.'

Carrie felt herself filling up. 'Will you be all right? What will you do for the rest of the evening?'

Heidi collapsed against the wall. 'Bed, that's where I'm heading.'

Carrie watched her reach unsteadily for her bed and creep under the covers. She wondered if she should stay, but she had to change now for the show, so decided she'd tell Brett and let him worry about it. She had enough on her mind if she was to get on that stage.

As she waited for the lift, a warm glow of happiness engulfed her and she felt more alive than she had in years. She was to appear on that stage in the most exquisite dress she had ever worn. Excitement and fear intermingled, but by the time she'd reached her cabin she was humming a catchy tune and could hardly stop her feet from keeping time with the beat.

★ ★ ★

The theme of the show was 'Dancing Round the World', with scenes from different countries. When the last number, a Hawaiian beach scene, concluded, the curtain fell, stage props were changed, and dancers positioned themselves for the final scene, which was set in the royal palace in Vienna. Carrie waited with Brett for the first strains of their Viennese waltz to begin. The dress fitted perfectly and, though she was now confident that she could take the performance in her stride, her pulse was racing.

Brett took her hand as they stepped onto the sweeping staircase that had been erected for them centre stage. Once in the dazzle of the lights, there was nothing for Carrie but the music and an audience she must give her all for.

★   ★   ★

Greg watched in a trance. He'd only managed to get in for the end of the show. But all he wanted to see was Carrie in that last scene. And now it was unfolding before his eyes. The set

195

was elaborate — the palace ballroom in Vienna. The dancers were dressed for a ball, standing round talking and drinking. All was gold and deep blue. The audience settled into a hushed silence before the orchestra began to play.

A beam of golden light focused on the top of a spiral staircase at the back of the stage. The other dancers watched in a trance as Carrie and Brett began to descend, her hand resting lightly on his arm. He had such a presence, in a tail coat and shiny patent shoes. She looked beautiful, a picture of elegance in a shimmering golden dress that skimmed her curves and swished out at her ankles in a cascade of glitter as she took each graceful step. Greg could sense a gasp from the audience as the couple swept onto the stage. The music changed. Greg recognised the tune: 'Edelweiss'. It would be perfect for Carrie. Gentle and happy. A lovely Viennese waltz.

Brett took Carrie in his arms and they began to float in the beam of golden light, so graceful, so beautiful. The audience was in thrall. Greg couldn't move. He couldn't take his eyes off her.

The other dancers began to join in until the whole cast was on stage for a wonderfully happy party scene. Then the curtain went down to rapturous applause.

But the audience were shouting for more. Greg sat rigid. Eventually the clapping subsided and the orchestra began to play a slow plaintive tune, quietly seductive. The curtain rose again, the audience silent and expectant. The stage was in darkness except for tiny brilliant stars. As a soft blue light deepened, Carrie and Brett could be seen standing alone in the centre, looking into each other eyes. They were very still.

A woman walked onto the side of the stage with a microphone held close to her mouth and began to sing 'Blue Moon'. Carrie and Brett began to move. Greg found he was holding his breath. He had never seen anything so moving. The music was soft and slow, the audience silent. Just two people in a pool of deep blue light performing the most exquisite dance he had ever seen. The rumba. The dance of love.

The music faded and an arc of brilliant white light framed Carrie and Brett at the back of the stage, hand in hand. The audience were on their feet. When the curtain finally went down, Greg remained seated until the theatre emptied, then slowly he walked back to his room.

* * *

It was much later when Greg found Carrie out on deck alone. He hadn't slept. He was still wearing his uniform; hadn't bothered to change, just sat in his room staring into space and trying to come to terms with what was happening to him.

Carrie had changed into a short summer dress and was leaning on the ship's rail, staring out across the sea. The pale pink lanterns which had been hung over the deck for the party earlier gave a gentle glow in the darkness of the night. Greg had only come out for a breath of air, not expecting to find anyone still up. He watched her for a while, wondering what to do. Should he go back inside? But even as he was thinking these thoughts, his steps were taking him closer to her as if he had no control over his actions.

'Back to Vancouver again tomorrow,' he said.

She turned in surprise, suddenly aware of him standing beside her.

'Are you looking forward to getting home?' he asked.

They were both looking out into the dark emptiness of the night and she couldn't see his face. But there was an uncertainty in his voice she hadn't heard before.

'I think so. This isn't real, is it?' She tried to make her own voice sound normal so that he wouldn't guess at the turmoil his closeness stirred in her.

'It's real for me.'

'Of course.'

'You didn't make it for dinner with me last night,' he said quietly.

'No, I couldn't let Tom down. He's looked after me all week.'

'And do you need looking after?' His voice was low and expressive, turning her stomach in knots.

She was aware that he was looking at her and turned to face him. 'No, but it's been nice.'

'And will you see Tom again when you get home?'

She tensed, wondering where this was leading, determined to keep her head. 'We plan to keep in touch. How about you? I expect you have some leave after this cruise.'

His laugh was hollow. 'No such luck. We turn the ship round with another load of passengers and off again.'

He took a step back from the rail and then moved closer to her. As his bare arm touched hers, she couldn't help an involuntary shiver.

'You were sensational tonight in that show,' he said.

She turned to him in surprise. 'You were there?'

'Of course. How could I miss seeing you dance?'

'How did you know?'

'Carrie, I know about most things that happen on my ship. As you reminded me once, it's my responsibility.'

She smiled, remembering. 'I had no idea we were going to do that rumba at the end. When the other dancers left the stage, Brett grabbed hold of me and then the curtain went up. I had no option but to follow him and dance.'

Greg laughed. 'The audience always call for an encore. They'd have felt cheated if you hadn't performed.'

Carrie frowned. 'So why didn't he tell me?'

'Because he didn't want you to run scared. He knew once you were up on that stage you could do it. And you did.'

Carrie shook her head in resignation. 'He was probably right. I didn't have time for nerves. One minute I was in a finale and feeling pleased I'd got through it without disgracing myself. Then I was dancing again in the full glare of a spotlight.'

'Brett and Heidi always do the rumba for that last encore. I've seen them do the most amazing routines. Heidi's a talented dancer. It's a shame they don't get on. They dance well together.'

'The audience would have been disappointed tonight then. We did a very basic routine.'

Greg shook his head. 'No, it was perfect in its simplicity. Anything more would have spoiled it.'

Carrie shrugged. He was being kind. She would have liked it to have been more spectacular, but they hadn't had time to rehearse or plan.

Greg pulled himself upright. 'I should have stopped it, you know.

Meryl wasn't happy about it. She thought it was all a bit risky, not knowing anything about you. And I was doubtful until Brett reassured me that you had done it all before.'

She looked at him. 'So why didn't you stop it?'

His expression softened. 'Because I wanted to see what you could do.' He hesitated. 'And I knew you wanted to do it.'

She could sense he wanted to take her in his arms and hold her close. And it was what she wanted with all her heart. But she had to be strong. If she gave in now, she would be lost. Her heart was so tight she could hardly breathe.

They were silent for a while as they watched the sea, inky black now. Then Greg straightened and Carrie turned to see if he was going to walk away. A sharp stab of pain clutched at her heart and she bit her lip to hold back the tears. He was going to leave her standing here alone, and she would never see him again.

But he stood a little way off, regarding her steadily. 'Will you come up to my room and have a drink with me?'

He hadn't meant to say any of that, but her closeness was overcoming all his reserves of willpower. He couldn't let her go. He had to keep her near him for as long as possible.

A huge wave of relief cast aside all her reservations. They were to have a little longer. She smiled up at him as he took her hand and led her to the lift.

She stood uncertainly as he unlocked the door to his apartment, not knowing what he would expect.

'Carrie, don't look so frightened. I asked you to join me for a drink so we can talk. That's all.'

His smile relaxed her and she followed him inside. It was a huge luxury apartment above the bridge deck, tastefully furnished in soft green and cream with long leather sofas arranged round a low table, an elaborate floral display at its centre. The thick carpet felt soft beneath her feet. Mirrors and paintings on the wall gave a homely feel. A huge desk stood in one corner strewn with papers, a laptop at its centre. Through an open connecting door she glimpsed a king-sized bed tastefully covered with regency stripe, and heavy drapes at the windows in complementary colours, layered over floaty white curtains.

'Bit different from my tiny cabin,' she said, staring round the room.

'This is my home for months on end. It's not so bad though,' he said.

He led her out through patio windows onto a balcony overlooking the sea. A round copper-topped table and two chairs stood near the ship's rail. Gentle ripples of moonlight glinting golden on the dark water; the sky a sheet of black velvet embedded with brilliant stars.

'Shall we go inside and have a drink?' Greg seemed a little uneasy, his manner less confident than usual, his expression less certain.

'Why don't we stay out here? It's a lovely evening,' she said.

He smiled his acquiescence and pulled out a chair at the table for her to sit on, then went inside. Soft light filtered from the room and music drifted out on the balmy night air. Carrie could hear Greg talking to someone, then he came out again and sat opposite to her. A few moments later a steward appeared with a bottle of champagne in a silver ice bucket. He put it on the table between them and produced two tall flute glasses, which he polished with the towel from his wrist; then he set them on the table. Greg thanked him and he departed.

Carrie watched as Greg popped the cork over the side of the ship. 'Do you ever drink anything but champagne?' she laughed, trying to ease the tension between them.

'Not unless I have to,' he quipped back, his face relaxing into a smile.

He handed a glass to her and they sat in quiet contemplation, sipping their champagne, enjoying being together, yet mindful of what was to come. Tomorrow she would be walking down the gangway, away from this ship, away from Greg. His look told her they were both having the same thoughts.

He broke the silence. 'Tell me about yourself, Carrie. Where do you come from? Why are you here alone?' He'd vowed he wouldn't go down this route, but he couldn't help himself. He wanted to know more about this woman who had so unexpectedly captured his heart.

Where to start? 'Well, you know all about my dancing career now, thanks to Brett.'

'But there's more than that, isn't there?'

She frowned.

'I think you've been hurt in the past, am I right?' he pressed.

She looked away. 'I really don't want to talk about it.'

He nodded. 'I thought so.'

'Why do you say that?'

'Because you're so wary of men. You don't want it to happen again.'

She sighed. 'Am I that transparent?'

'Carrie, I'm only trying to understand you. Can't we just talk and enjoy each other's company for a while?'

'I'm sorry. It's just the way I am.' Then suddenly she wanted to talk, to tell him everything. 'When my mum became ill my boyfriend couldn't cope with it. He left me. I never want to feel that hurt again.'

Greg took her hand across the table. 'I'm sorry, I shouldn't have probed.'

Why was she baring her soul like this? She had to change the subject before she made a fool of herself. She'd almost given him her life history now, yet she knew nothing of his.

'The stars are so much brighter here,' she mused, looking up towards the sky, trying desperately to keep her voice steady.

'No light pollution, that's the reason.

We're in the Pacific Ocean.' His voice had taken on a lighter tone, yet the atmosphere was still highly charged.

Holding Carrie's hand, he pulled her from her seat and slipped his arms round her. They stood for a few moments, lulled by the ship's steady motion and the gentle lapping of waves against her side.

'Shall we go inside?' he whispered into her hair.

She followed him in, and this time his arms enfolded her. She didn't pull away but relaxed into him. The voice of Michael Buble singing 'The Way You Look Tonight' filled the room as he stood looking down at her.

'I want to kiss you so much, but I don't want to frighten you away,' Greg whispered.

She leaned in towards him, and he drew her close and brushed her lips softly. As his kisses became more urgent, she relaxed into his arms, and nothing mattered anymore but being with this man in this moment.

When they drew apart, his eyes were heavy with desire. 'I've been wanting to do that since I first set eyes on you.'

The gentle lyrics of 'Hold Me Close' floated on the air. Greg pulled her into his arms again and, as they swayed slowly to the music, she felt she was floating on air.

When the song finished, Greg took her hand. 'I'll take you up into the bow of the ship. You'll like it up there.'

Carrie followed him along the deck, up ladders and along other decks, alongside lifeboats, and then they were clambering over ropes right into the bow of the ship.

Standing there, with the wind in her hair, she began to understand how men like Greg felt about the sea and the ships they sailed. The only sound was the gentle splash of bow waves skimming the sides of the ship in the darkness; above, the huge expanse of the universe was brilliant with stars. Alone, side by side, very close, Carrie felt she was experiencing true happiness for the first time. If only it could be like this forever.

Greg turned to her. Their eyes met, and his expression was unbearably tender and full of an unspoken longing to match her own. He took her in his arms again and kissed her gently at first, and then with great passion. The world receded. And Carrie knew she was deeply in love.

As they strolled back along the deck, music floated in the air as all areas of the ship were partying for the last night on board. Carrie could hear the strains of 'Blue Moon' coming from somewhere inside the ship. She looked up into the deep dark sky and Greg followed her gaze. Then he took her in his arms as they danced slowly round the deck beneath a perfect crescent moon.

The music stopped and Greg squeezed her hand tightly. 'The night isn't over yet,' he said, and she knew where they were heading.

9

A Shoulder to Cry On

The ballroom was packed and there was hardly room to squeeze onto the floor. They didn't attempt to dance, just swayed like everyone else to the rhythm of the music and slowly merged with other couples as the band played 'You're Once, Twice, Three Times a Lady'.

As Greg held Carrie close, she was full of love yet near to tears. They didn't speak, just clung together and moved round the floor, each cherishing this moment of closeness. When the music stopped, Greg led her to the side and stood gazing down at her.

'You're off in the morning,' he said.

'Yes, my case is packed.'

'I'll miss our dances.'

'I'll miss you.' She tried to smile but

her heart was heavy.

'Me, too.'

He put an arm round her shoulder and they watched for a few moments as dancers swirled round the floor. Most of them would be going home together, and Carrie envied them. The ballroom was bathed in golden light and she thought she had never seen a room more beautiful.

Greg took her in his arms as the band began to play 'Somewhere Over the Rainbow'. Love and longing were surging through her as they began a slow foxtrot round the dance floor. When the music came to an end, Greg stood away from her and his eyes held a world of sadness.

'Do you want me to see you back to your room?' His smile faltered.

Carrie was finding it difficult to breathe. This really was the end. She shook her head, unable to form any words, knowing only that she did not want to be alone in her room.

He nodded. 'Take care, Carrie. I

hope your dreams come true.' He wound his arms round her waist and brushed her lips gently. For an eternity — or maybe a second — he held her, then turned and left.

Carrie stared after him. She wanted to stop him leaving, but what would be the use? Her chin began to wobble and her heart grew tight as she watched him walk away. It seemed like the bottom had suddenly dropped out of her world. When she felt her legs would carry her, she rushed back to her room, not wanting anyone to see the tears streaming down her face. Once safely behind her closed door, she threw herself onto her bed and sobbed all her pain into the soft covers.

Then she got up, telling herself firmly that it had been a holiday romance and now it was over. She put on more make-up and went in search of Tom, hoping he would not have already gone to bed. She needed his reassuring presence to get her through the next few hours. Then she would be down that gangway and on firm land again.

With a great feeling of relief, she found him sitting in the Seaview Lounge having a nightcap before retiring to his cabin for the night. He put down his glass and gave her a searching look as she slumped onto the sofa beside him.

'Now what?' he said.

'Tom, I don't want to talk about it. I want you to talk to me about anything other than Greg. Please!'

He shook his head and sighed. 'Okay, are you happy to be going home?'

'Yes, definitely. I want to get back into my routine and put this week behind me.'

'But I think we've both found something special this week.' His look was questioning.

An overwhelming tiredness was consuming her. 'I wish I hadn't.'

'It hurts, doesn't it?'

She nodded miserably. If only she could tell him she loved him. She knew it was what he wanted, and it would have taken all the hurt away for both of them. But they both knew that wasn't possible.

She averted her gaze. 'I'm sorry.'

'Don't be, Carrie. You've found what you want. Don't throw it away.'

She shook her head, all her fight gone. 'He has his life here in Vancouver. I have mine back home. Our paths won't cross again. Why can't life work out better?'

He took her hand in his and gave her a concerned look. 'You can make it work out better if you want it to.'

She turned to him. 'How can I?'

'You both love each other. That's all it takes.'

'No, Tom, it isn't. And anyway, we haven't got that far. We've only had this week. It takes a lot longer than that.'

'I don't think so. I think when you meet the right person, you know straight away.'

She could tell by his look what this was costing him. Yet he was encouraging her to stay with Greg. 'Tom, I'm going home.'

* ★ ★

Dawn was already breaking when Carrie got back to her cabin. She sat for a while slumped on the end of the bed, knowing it was pointless to try to sleep. After a while she ambled out onto the deck for one last glimpse of the mountains and sea before they docked. She wanted to cry her sorrow into that deep grey sea, yet felt she had no more tears to shed, just an empty feeling of loss.

How had she allowed this to happen? Before she'd met Greg she'd been content, free and optimistic for her future. Now she was filled with longings and desires, and the lonely future that stretched ahead filled her with dread. She knew she wouldn't see Greg again. He would be up on the bridge when they docked and they'd said their good-byes last night. All she wanted now was to get down that gangway and as far away from the ship as she could, with all its memories and heartache.

Once they docked, the gangway was
soon in place and the luggage on its
way to the waiting coach that would
take them to the hotel. Carrie wished
they were going straight to the airport
instead of another two days in Vancouver before that happened.

She was halfway down the gangway
when she heard footsteps behind her.
Then she heard a voice calling her
name, a voice that made her heart stop,
and she turned slowly to see Greg
hurrying down after her. He looked
dishevelled and anguished, his face
drawn and grey, not at all his usual
composed self, yet more handsome
than ever. He eased himself ahead of
her and stopped any further progress.

Other passengers were trying to
disembark and she and Greg were
causing a holdup. It was the last thing
Carrie wanted. Last night in the
ballroom had been the most painful
experience she could remember. She

didn't want a repeat.

Greg realised the confusion he was causing and eased her to one side so that others could pass. 'Carrie,' he said softly, his mouth hardly able to form the words.

Tears were pouring down her face. Every fibre of her body wanted to reach out and pull him to her and lose herself in the warmth of his love. Instead she stood rigid, vaguely aware of people looking at her with some concern.

Then she felt him place something in her hand. 'It's the key to my house and the address. Please stay there until I get back.'

She stared at him, a lump forming in her throat that prevented her from saying anything. His pleading eyes were tearing her apart.

'Please. I'll be back next Saturday and then I'll get a week off.'

She made herself look straight at him, and through tight lips managed a shaky response. 'Greg, I have a flight home the day after tomorrow.'

'But you could stay the extra two weeks. Lots of people do.'

They were being jostled by impatient passengers wanting to get down the gangway. He squeezed up against her so that people could pass and was now standing so close she could feel the warmth of his body pressed against her.

'Carrie, we can't throw this away. I've never felt like this before. And I know you feel it too.' There was desperation in his face and his voice.

She shook her head. 'We can't, Greg.'

'We can,' he insisted. She could hear the break in his voice, the effort he was making to keep her with him.

She wanted him to enfold her in his arms and make the hurt go away. But it was becoming impossible to keep their position any longer. The surge down the gangway was tearing them apart. She was being pushed downwards and he was being left further and further away. Still their eyes held each other. His despairing look was breaking her heart. With one superhuman effort she turned and continued down, the pain cutting through her almost unbearable.

Tom had saved her a seat on the coach and stood up to let her get on the inside. She slithered in with tears running down her face. He eased himself into the seat beside her, and after handing her a handkerchief he took her hand.

She tried to speak but the words refused to form on her tongue, so she buried her face in his shoulder and wept. He rested his head against hers to comfort her. Then she realised she had the key gripped tightly in her hand.

★   ★   ★

The coach stopped on Granville Island for a couple of hours en route to the hotel. It was Canada Day and the waterfront was alive with every type of craft. Tiny pugwash boats were giving round trips of the harbour, all the cafés were full, street markets were bustling, and there were entertainers on every corner. One whisked off Tom's hat and juggled with it before returning it to his head like a flying saucer. He laughed and Carrie tried to join in the merriment, but her heart refused to budge.

There was a lovely welcome at the hotel, with a large bowl of punch and plates of cookies set out in the reception area. Tom did his best to cheer Carrie up, and finally she began to relax. The worst was over. Now she had to concentrate on the present.

After a quick change in her room, she met Tom at the bar, where he was slaking his thirst with a large glass of beer. He ordered a white wine for her as she perched on a bar stool beside him. The bar was spacious, with tall windows draped in rich taffeta curtains. Crystal chandeliers were reflected in mirrors on every wall, and soft music filtered from loudspeakers. As she sat sipping her wine, Carrie felt her mind settle. She had been so lucky to have met Tom. Without him, she didn't think she could have coped with any of it. He was a lovely man, warm and kind, and he was still here beside her. They could spend the next two days together and the flight home. And they could meet up again after that if she wanted to. She shook herself. She'd been silly mooning over Greg. He was way out of her reach. Tom was here and now.

She reached out, put a hand on his arm and gave him an affectionate smile. He looked surprised and put his hand over hers. Slowly the pain in her heart began to seep away. It had been an episode of utter madness, one she had been lucky to escape unscathed.

'Do you want to eat here in the hotel, or shall we find somewhere in town?' Tom asked, still holding her hand and smiling at her.

'I'd like to explore the town.'

'Me, too,' he said, sliding off the bar stool.

They made their way down to the seafront and walked along the promenade, watching the activity on the beach. The sun was sinking low over the dark mountains, and along the promenade skyscrapers stood silhouetted against the deepening blue of a twilight sky. Groups of people were picnicking and playing guitars. Jugglers and magicians performed to small clusters who'd gathered round to watch. Waves lapped the sand.

The carnival atmosphere began to affect them both. Tom put an arm round Carrie's waist as they strolled along, watching all the activity. Eventually they found a cosy place to eat, and Carrie felt more relaxed than she had in days. She almost began to believe that she could bury the pain and move on. She'd done it once all those years ago, and now she'd do it again.

They were sitting opposite each other in a candle-lit corner of the tiny bistro with soft music playing, and had lapsed into an easy silence as they ate their meal. Carrie looked up to see Tom scrutinising her face.

'Tom, you don't have to look after

me all the time.'

'I want to.'

'But you should be mixing with other people or going off on your own, doing whatever you want to do.'

'Carrie, I want to be with you.'

★   ★   ★

They were on the coach the next morning at nine o'clock for a tour of the city of Vancouver. Everywhere was colourful and lively. Chinatown was regaled in bunting, with bustling markets. The Japanese district was full of restaurants embellished in red and gold. Upmarket shopping streets lay side by side with rundown areas where nobody ventured after dark.

'Look at that huge building,' Tom said, leaning over Carrie to point out of the coach window. 'I've read about it. It's supported so that when there's an earthquake it just rocks gently.'

Carrie stiffened. 'Do they have earthquakes here very often?'

'I believe so.'

'Well, I hope they don't have one while we're here,' she said.

He laughed. 'I shouldn't worry. All the buildings are proofed against them. And we've only got until tomorrow to worry about.'

Carrie tried not to think about tomorrow. Here with Tom she was coping. Once back home she wasn't so sure she would.

Tom was pointing out the ancient steam clock as it puffed out its vapour. Skyscrapers constructed from brass and glass towered above them. Old and new sat side by side. Sea planes dipped overhead on their descent into the water. The whole city was alive and vibrant, and Carrie loved it.

That evening they went back to the bistro they'd visited the night before. In the same quiet corner, with just the glow of a small candle, Carrie fell silent. Tomorrow they were to leave Canada and fly home.

Tom picked up on her mood and

gave her a concerned look. 'I can't bear to see you so sad,' he said.

She couldn't check the tears any longer. 'I'm sorry, Tom. I didn't want to spoil our last night.'

His frown deepened. 'You don't have to do this.'

She looked at him through watery eyes. 'Do what?'

He looked down at his plate. Then, after contemplating for a moment, he took a deep breath and gave her a searching look. 'You don't have to leave tomorrow. You could stay on.'

Her eyes opened wide. 'Tom, what are you talking about?'

'I'm talking about you and Greg.'

She shook her head violently. 'No, I'm over that. I don't want to talk about it. Please, Tom, leave it. I mean it. I don't want you to ever mention it again.' She took a deep breath to calm herself. 'I'm sad because our holiday is over and I've enjoyed being with you.'

'Carrie, stop it. We can stay friends.'

'But will I see you again?' she asked

him earnestly. It was suddenly vitally important that she did.

He squeezed her hand gently across the table and smiled. 'As often as you want.' Then his expression changed. 'But I'm not talking about you and me.'

She looked down and in a small voice said, 'I know.'

He bent his head and considered for a moment, then faced her, waiting for her to look up at him. 'Carrie, you don't have to go home tomorrow. You could stay here until Greg gets back.'

She stared at him, speechless.

'Several of the people who came with us are staying on here for the extra two weeks. Maybe you could do the same.'

'Why would I do that?'

'Because you're in love with Greg.'

Carrie felt her throat constrict. She couldn't breathe. All she wanted was to go back to the hotel and bury her head in the pillow and shut out all the pain. Tom watched silently until she eventually gained some control over her voice.

'Tom, I can't. My brother will be at

the airport to meet me. And Julia is expecting me to start work with her next week.'

'I think they'd understand if you explained,' he said gently.

'But I'd be letting Julia down.'

'If you go back home now you'll be letting yourself down.'

'But I don't know that he loves me.'

'He's asked you to stay, hasn't he? And he's given you the key to his house. That's pretty convincing.'

She frowned. 'Why did he do that? If I was staying on, I'd stay in the hotel like all the others.'

'I think it was his way of telling you how he felt about you.'

She shook her head. 'But what if it all goes wrong?'

'Then you'll go home and pick up the pieces. It's what we have to do.'

She looked at him through tearful eyes.

'Sometimes you have to go out on a limb and risk everything, Carrie. It's the only way you will ever know.'

Still she said nothing.

'Carrie, don't turn your back on this. Greg will be back in another five days. See how you feel then. Otherwise you'll always wonder what could have been.'

She knew Tom was right, and suddenly she knew she wanted to do what he was suggesting. She had to know whether what she and Greg had was real. She had to stay and wait for him. A lightness filled her. Whatever it took, she'd do it.

Then panic took over. 'Where do I start? I know it was an option when I booked. But I can't change my mind just like that and stay on now.'

'Look, let's ask the rep in the morning, then we'll take it from there.'

She felt herself slump. 'It can't be done, Tom.'

He shook his head dismissively. 'If they have a seat on the plane, then I don't see why not. We have all day tomorrow. The flight isn't till late. I'll help you. I'll be with you every step of the way.'

'Oh, Tom, will you really do that for me?' She hesitated. 'But it's the last day of your holiday. You'll miss the trip to the Butchart Gardens.'

'I don't care about the gardens. But I do care about you.'

Suddenly she was laughing and crying all at the same time and didn't care who saw her. Maybe the option to stay on was still open to her. She would have a little longer in this wonderful city. She would see Greg again.

She took Tom's hand in both of hers. 'Tom, thank you, thank you.'

⋆　⋆　⋆

It took the whole of the next day to sort out. Tom was as good as his word and did everything he could to help her. After enquiring, they found there was a spare seat on the plane at the later date. All it would cost was the extra time in the hotel.

Once the euphoria subsided, doubts began to creep in. What would happen after her week with Greg?

'I'm not sure I should be doing this. It's not going to lead anywhere,' she told Tom as they sat having a final cup of coffee before he left.

'You have to do it, Carrie,' he said.

'But I can't stay here forever.'

Tom put a steadying hand on her arm. 'Carrie, you are not staying here forever. You are simply prolonging your holiday. Then when you've seen Greg again you can decide. There'll be a *lot* to decide. But Greg wants you to be here when he gets back. And you want to be here. If you go home now, you'll never see him again. Is that what you really want?'

'No,' she said, not looking at him. The thought of leaving without seeing Greg again now seemed unbearable.

'Then stop worrying. See what happens when you meet up. Then you can go home as planned. Nothing will be lost. At least you'll know.'

Know what? She knew she loved Greg. She wasn't sure how he felt about her. Maybe he just wanted her company for a few days when he was on leave. But deep down she knew it was more than this. It didn't make it any easier.

★ ★ ★

Finally Carrie was left in the hotel lounge after waving the coach a sad farewell. She felt a clutch of fear now Tom had gone. What would happen when Greg returned? Where did they go from here? He'd said they had something special, but she knew she must not read too much into it. She had no idea what he was expecting, only that he had wanted her to stay and spend some time with him. But she wasn't going to think about any of that now. She'd made her decision, so all she could do was wait and see.

Back in her room she phoned her brother, Neil, and told him of her change of plans. He was delighted and told her that after travelling so far it was silly not to make the best of it.

'You deserve it, after everything you gave up to care for Mum,' he said.

She felt a lump in her throat. It was what her mum would have wanted, she knew.

Julia was fine with it, too, and told her that Marie, the dance teacher who was helping out, would be more than happy to stay on as long as necessary. 'I think she'd like the job permanently,' Julia joked. 'But don't worry. She's not getting it.'

Five more days and Greg would be with her. During that time she could wander and explore this wonderfully exciting city of Vancouver. But first she was going to see where he lived. The key was tucked away in the pocket of her suitcase. Attached was a label with an address on it. Tomorrow she would go and find it. Greg had told her to stay there and wait for his return. She wouldn't do that, but there was no harm in looking. It would give her some clue to the man she was waiting for, the man she had cancelled her flight home for and put her life on hold for.

*   *   *

After enquiring at reception the next morning, Carrie discovered the house was on Vancouver Island, which was separated from the mainland by a stretch of water. A pleasant woman of about fifty stood behind the desk, explained how to get there, and warned her that it would be a long day.

This didn't deter Carrie. She needed something to calm her mind and put aside her doubts, if only for one day. With her bag strung over her shoulder and a map clutched in her hand, she stepped out into the busy street. The sun was hot, and as she she pulled out her sun hat and glasses she wondered if she should have put on a long-sleeved shirt to protect herself from its rays.

She managed to get to the ferry and bought her ticket. The crossing was calm with a cooling breeze. Standing on the deck, surrounded by water and with the wind in her hair, she felt closer to Greg, and it seemed no time before she was disembarking on the island.

The waterfront was crowded with people dressed in tribal costumes. It must have been a special day. Stalls selling beaded jewellery, dream catchers and other traditional gifts lined the streets. Carrie stopped to stare at what she thought was the statue of a man dressed all in white, but when a child put a coin in the cap at his feet he suddenly became animated. A trumpeter played a catchy tune. Along the opposite side of the wide paved waterfront were neatly laid gardens, and behind these, majestic hotels. Families were enjoying the summer sunshine and children ran around on the beach, one chasing a dog who kept running in and out of the water. Carrie ached to be part of it all, to have someone to share her life with, someone for whom she would always be special.

After asking for directions, she realised Greg's house was much further along the coast than it looked on the map. But she was enjoying the fresh air and sunshine as she happily strode along where she'd been told to go.

Once out of the touristy bit, the road began to wind around beautiful houses with breath-taking sea views, eventually giving way to a track through trees.

Then she saw it, standing on a rocky outcrop nestling within palm trees: a long low building, white and dazzling in the midday sun, with an indoor swimming pool stretching out from one end. An Audi stood in the drive.

The name on the white stucco wall matched the one on the label attached to the key. This was where Greg lived. This was where he'd told her to stay. A cold chill made her skin prickle. She couldn't believe what she was staring at. Between the trees was a view of the sea, its surface sparkling in the sunlight.

10

An Intruder Appears

A movement in front of the house caught Carrie's eye and she dodged behind a tree. A man ambled across the gravel with a wheelbarrow. He collected some logs, filled the barrow and then wheeled it down the side of the house. Carrie was still holding her breath when he reappeared and went over to a truck parked on the gravel, got in and drove up the track she had just come down. He must have been a gardener.

After standing there a few moments to steady her nerves, she crept up to the front door and tapped lightly on the big brass knocker. Nothing happened. She tried again. Then she walked all the way round the outside of the house peering in through the windows. The rooms were spacious, elegantly furnished in cool neutral colours with big picture windows to take advantage of the view.

It seemed that nobody was around. Well, Greg was hardly likely to give her a key to a house where someone else lived. The thought emboldened her to have a look inside. It was what she'd come for, what Greg had given her the key for. But she hadn't expected to find this.

Cautiously she put the key in the lock and the door swung open. It was cool and quiet inside the huge entrance hall with rooms leading off in all directions. There was large airy lounge at the back of the house, furnished with cream leather sofas round a low glass-topped table in front of a patio window. She pulled the blinds aside and gawped at pristine lawns stretching out to a summerhouse the size of a small bungalow.

As she progressed from room to room, she began to feel increasingly uneasy. The front room, with views across the bay, was laid out formally as a dining room, the furnishings stylish and expensive-looking. There was a wood-burning stove in the kitchen and great expanses of wall units. The bedroom was huge, with window drapes that complemented the cool blues and creams of the king-sized bed.

Then she found a smaller room that had a completely different feel to it. It was cosy and intimate. One wall was shelved from floor to ceiling and filled with books. An expensive-looking music system was set on a low cabinet, and a desk with a computer stood beside it. The walls here were covered in paintings. Carrie eased out a canvas from a pile stacked down the side of the desk. It was one Greg had done, a yacht at sea with the wind in its sails. He was a talented artist. She loved the way he'd captured the feel of the elements.

Sinking into the big leather chair, she tried to imagine Greg living in this house. Why did he need a place this size? And why were all the paintings in this small room, when he could have displayed them to much better effect if he'd spread them round the cream walls in the rest of the house?

Deep in her heart she knew she had made a mistake getting involved with him. The whole cruise thing had unbalanced her judgement. She should have gone home with Tom instead of swanning around in a strange country waiting for a man she knew nothing about.

She let herself out, quietly closed and locked the door, then walked thoughtfully back down the path. This wasn't her world. She longed for Tom to be there to comfort her, to bring some sort of normality back into her life.

After scrambling down onto the beach, she found a quiet sandy cove and perched on a jutting rock. It was cooler in the shade and gradually the rhythm of the sea gently lapping the rocks soothed her. She chided herself for her stupidity and wished she'd gone back with Tom yesterday. But she was stuck here now and would have to go through with it.

Finally she got up and made her way back to the seafront. But this time she didn't see the lively scene around her. All that was in her mind was a huge house and a man who had turned her head. And she wondered how she could possibly have allowed this to happen.

★　★　★

Back at the hotel and safely in her room, Carrie flopped into the chair and stared down across the city. Lights were beginning to twinkle below, but she was too weary and disheartened to appreciate their magic. It was only as she lay in bed hoping for the oblivion of sleep that visions of Greg and their brief moments together invaded her thoughts: their last evening together, the way he'd danced with her and held her and kissed her, the distraught way he'd looked at her when he'd placed the key in her hand only days ago, the urgency in his voice. She remembered how she had felt as she'd walked down the gangway away from him, and the relief when Tom had persuaded her to stay.

Did it really matter what sort of a house he had? It was the man that mattered. She had fallen in love with Greg and there was no denying it. And his feelings for her must have run deep or he wouldn't have asked such an enormous thing of her. He'd be back in a couple more days. They could spend some time together as planned. Then she could go home and continue her life. Despite telling herself over and over again how foolishly she was behaving, she knew she still wanted to wait for him.

She decided that she loved Vancouver. It was clean and bright and full of life, with bars and cafés everywhere. The whole city had a multicultural vibrancy, with young people working and playing and living life to the full. She'd sat for hours at pavement cafés watching people, and she did a lot of thinking. But the more she thought, the more she worried that she should not be waiting for Greg. All they would have was a few more days, and then what? More pain — the one thing she had avoided successfully for so many years. Nothing could come of their relationship. Their worlds were as far apart as it was possible to be. What had she been thinking when she'd let Tom go off without her and stayed here alone?

Yet, despite this, the excitement would grow when she thought of seeing Greg again. However long they could have together was worth all the hurt. It was as if some fever had possessed her mind, driving out common sense. She had to feel his arms around her and his lips touching hers just once more. Round and round in her head these thoughts would tumble, until she gave up and just walked and watched and envied the apparent simplicity of other people's lives.

★　★　★

The day before Greg was due to berth in Vancouver, Carrie couldn't settle. Finally she knew she had to go back to the island and have another look at his house. It couldn't do any harm, and she might see it differently now she'd got over the shock.

She set off for the ferry, feeling more confident this time. It was going to be a long and tiring day, but it was exactly what she needed. It gave her a purpose, and that was far better than wandering round aimlessly in a state of nervous tension.

Once back on the waterfront, and knowing exactly what lay before her, she took a moment to watch children running in and out of the sea on the beach before beginning the long walk to Greg's house. This time the track seemed less daunting now that she knew what lay at the end of it. There was nothing to fear. It was an empty house — one she'd been given the key to; one that Greg had pleaded with her to stay in.

The sight of it shimmering in the sunshine didn't shock her this time, and she could appreciate its beauty — the red slated roof, the palm trees wafting gently in the breeze against an azure sky. There was a rock garden set into the gravel in front with a pool of cool, clear water and giant carp swimming in and out of water lilies. If she saw the gardener today, she'd talk to him and try to explain who she was so he wouldn't think she was sneaking around and up to no good. It would be nice to sit for a while looking out over the terraces and then maybe wander round the garden. Or she could go into the little snug and play some music. Greg would be pleased she'd taken him up on his offer and spent some time at his house, even though she had stayed in the hotel.

She let herself in through the front door and made straight for the back room. Then a thought struck her. The whole place was like a show-house, hardly lived in. Maybe he had a housekeeper. He hadn't mentioned one. But then he hadn't had time to explain anything; had just pressed the key into her hand. She put the thought out of her mind. Greg had given her the key.

The room was cool, with the blinds closed as before. She drew them across to let the sunlight in.

Her body stiffened. Her heart stopped. The flurry of excitement she had felt was crushed instantly. She backed away and eased herself into a chair, the blood draining from her head and her legs useless.

Sitting on a lounger stretched out in the sun was a woman. She was dressed in a skimpy bikini and wore large dark glasses. Beside her on a low table were all the accoutrements necessary for a leisurely day in the garden: a bottle of water, a book, a big bag on the ground beside her. Her head was resting back as if she were sleeping. And she was certainly not the housekeeper.

Carrie gripped the arms of the chair

in a daze. She didn't know what to do. Yes, she did. She had to get out of here, and fast. Scrambling to her feet, she hoped her shaky legs would support her.

The woman turned to pick up her book. Carrie crouched back until the woman turned away again. Then she somehow got to the front door, shut it quietly behind her, and ran until she was down in the cove where she'd sat yesterday, out of sight of the house. Then she stopped for breath.

Her heart was thumping as she scrambled further along the beach and found a quiet spot to rest. Sitting rigid on a large smooth stone, she stared out over the sea and took deep breaths to try to steady her thumping heart. The sun was burning into her arms, yet she was shivering. What had she got herself into? Why had Greg done this to her? Why had he given her a key to a house where he lived with another woman? She needed to talk to someone. Pulling her phone from the pocket of her shorts, she dialled the only number where she knew she could get help.

Tom's voice calmed her. 'Carrie, how lovely to hear from you. How's it going?'

'Tom, it isn't.'

His tone changed. 'Come on, tell me.'

'I went to his house and he's got another woman there. She was sitting in the garden and I rushed out and now I'm sitting on the beach and I don't know what to do. Why would he do that to me, Tom?' She knew she was gabbling but that was why she'd rung Tom, because she knew she could and that he would understand.

When she'd stopped for breath his voice came over calm and steady. 'Carrie, stop a minute. You're not making a lot of sense.'

Again she began blurting out her feelings. 'Nothing makes sense. And he's got this huge house on a cliff overlooking the sea. Why would he have a house like that just for himself when he says he's hardly ever at home?'

'Why shouldn't he? He obviously earns enough to afford it.'

'But nothing about him is real. He keeps playing with my feelings and I keep falling for it. I thought he loved me but all he does is tell me lies. And it hurts so much. I wish you were here. I'm all on my own and I'm lonely. I was so looking forward to him coming tomorrow, and now this. I'm sorry, Tom. You don't want to hear all this. But I had to talk to someone and it had to be you.'

Tom waited patiently until she'd run out of breath and come to a stop. 'Right, then let's take this one step at a time. How do you know this woman lives there with him?' he said.

'Well, why would she be there if she didn't? She looked well installed to me on her lounger with her book.'

'OK, that does sound odd, I agree. Have you tried to contact Greg?'

She was hesitant. 'No, I wouldn't know how.'

'You said he lies to you all the time. What lies has he told you?'

'He never told me anything about himself and I didn't even know who he was for two days. That was deceitful.'

'No it wasn't, Carrie. He wasn't lying about anything. He just wanted to be himself for a while, and he explained that to you. And did you ask him anything about himself?'

'No, not really.'

'Then you should be pleased that he wanted to talk about you. That shows he was more interested in you than in himself. Always a good quality in anyone, I'd say.'

'You liked him, didn't you?' she said in a small voice.

'I think you ought to give him a chance to explain.'

He paused, but she could think of nothing more to say. Then his voice came again, kind and reassuring. 'Carrie, when you come home I'll be there for you. You won't be alone.'

'Thank you.'

She couldn't stop shaking as she stuffed the phone back in her pocket. With a heavy heart she got up and began to make her way back towards the waterfront. The sun was low in the sky, the beach quiet now. People would be going home to relax and eat. Later on, others would be out enjoying the cool of the evening. And she would be sitting in her lonely hotel room, her mind in turmoil, waiting for a man she no longer trusted. She cursed herself for being so weak, for letting Tom persuade her to give Greg the benefit of the doubt. Yet she knew deep down it was her own choice, something she had to do.

She stopped dead in her tracks. She was not going to hang around waiting for Greg's explanations. She was going back to that house, and she would confront that woman and find out the truth.

Once she'd made the decision she felt stronger, more composed. But she had to get back there quickly before her courage failed her. In her present mood she could tackle it. She couldn't hurt more than she did at the moment. That, mixed with anger, strengthened her resolve.

She raced back along the waterfront and on to the track leading to the house. She was hot and panting for breath, but she carried on until she was standing in front of it again. Then her pace slowed and her hands became clammy. She wanted to turn and run, but her feet were firmly anchored to the gravel.

The white walls had taken on a mellow pink glow in the late-afternoon sun and looked quite beautiful. She took a moment to steady her breathing, then straightened up and strode round the side of the house to the back garden.

The woman was standing folding the lounger. She'd slipped a colourful sarong over her bikini and pushed her sunglasses on top of her dark curly hair. Carrie stood watching as she gathered her things together in her bag and then straightened and turned, giving Carrie a questioning look.

'Hello, can I help you?' she drawled.

'I don't know,' Carrie snapped.

The woman raised an eyebrow. She was quite big, with strong features, and looked older close up. Probably in her late thirties, and darkly tanned with bright red lips.

'Do you mind me asking who you are?' Carrie said in a steady voice.

The woman's expression hardened. 'Yes, I do mind. But maybe you'd like to tell me who you are.'

'I've been given the key to this property and I wasn't expecting there to be anyone here.'

The woman gave a hollow laugh as she slipped her feet into pink strappy sandals. 'Dear old Greg. So he gave you a key, did he?'

Carrie was losing confidence in the presence of this older woman who seemed to feel she had every right to be there.

The woman was studying her. 'And why did he do that?'

'Is it any of your business?' Carrie managed, determined not to be intimidated.

The woman was beginning to look annoyed. 'As a matter of fact, yes it is. This happened to be my home. Until he changed the locks, that is. I don't suppose he's told you about me. I should ask him if I were you, before you get too involved.'

Carrie felt her face blanch and a cold shiver of fear ran down her spine. 'I'm sorry, I didn't know,' she mumbled without looking up.

'There will be a lot of things you don't know about Greg, dear,' the woman said, as she continued to pack her things away. 'I don't suppose he told you that I transformed this house into what you see today. That was while he was swanning round the world on his cruise ships living it up.'

Anger shot through Carrie, but she knew she must not let this woman see how upset she was. 'It's his job,' she said sharply, her head snapping up to face her.

The woman looked at her in surprise. 'Well, it wasn't a lot of fun for me, I can tell you. He wouldn't give it up and get a proper job; one that allowed him to come home at night and be a proper husband.'

'Are you two married?' Carrie asked.

She could tell the woman was thrown by this but she recovered quickly. 'That is none of your business. All I'll say is steer clear of him; that's my advice to you.' She continued to fold the lounger, then stopped and laid it on the grass again. 'I'll leave this out for you. Put it back in the summerhouse when you've finished.' With that, she picked up her bag and walked round the side of the house, leaving Carrie staring at the spot where she'd been sitting.

Once she was sure the woman had gone, Carrie walked slowly back out to the track and along to the waterfront. The children had gone from the beach, and the waterfront was deserted except for a few couples sauntering along enjoying the last bit of sunshine. She wandered down onto the sand in search of somewhere she could perch, somewhere she could be alone with her thoughts, and found an old bit of driftwood. She couldn't go back to the hotel just yet. The walls of the room would press in on her.

A man was throwing a ball for his dog. Waves gently washed the shore, their rhythm soothing as they rippled over the sand. Carrie had no idea how long she sat there staring out, her mind numb. But as the sun began to sink low towards the sea, she knew she had to get back.

Stiffly she got up and slowly made her way back to the ferry. The crossing was smooth, the water a sheet of crimson velvet with only the bow waves of the ferry breaking its surface. When the twinkling lights of the harbour came into view, she wished she could have been watching them with Greg. But that wasn't going to happen, not now. Not now that she knew how Greg had deceived her. With a heavy heart, she got off the ferry when it berthed and made her way slowly back to the hotel.

Once inside the hotel room with the door firmly closed behind her, she flopped onto the bed. When she felt she had poured every emotion she had into her pillow she sat up, shook herself and slowly got off the bed.

Well, that was it. Tomorrow she'd go off on the coach trip that had been organised to take anyone who wanted to go to a local market. That way Greg wouldn't be able to find her. She was determined to enjoy the rest of her stay and put him completely out of her mind. It was what she should have done when she left the ship. She'd phone Tom tomorrow and tell him what had happened; tonight she didn't have the energy. She undressed, threw her clothes into an untidy pile on the chair, snuggled beneath the quilt and fell immediately into an exhausted sleep.

The phone ringing on her bedside table woke Carrie, and she struggled out of sleep to look at the clock. It was midday. She picked up the receiver. It was reception.

'We have a Captain Winton here asking to speak to you.'

Carrie was fully awake. 'No, it's not convenient at the moment,' she shouted down the phone.

'Shall I give him a message?' the receptionist persisted.

'No, no message.'

She put the phone down before any awkward questions could be asked, then sat up in bed in a daze and tried to stop shaking. She should have been up hours ago. The coach to the market would leave without her if she didn't hurry. And Greg was here in the hotel. She hoped he'd give up and go. If he was still there when she got down, she'd tell him to leave her alone and that she never wanted to see him again.

Within an hour she was showered and ready to go. Nervously she made her way down to reception.

As soon as the lift door opened she saw him. It was as if someone had flicked a switch and, despite her misgivings, her world lit up. Standing there, tall and straight, he was watching for her. He looked fresh and cool in an open-necked shirt and chinos, his tanned face as handsome as ever, his smile still twisting her heart. She took a deep breath and with enormous self-will forced herself to take control of her feelings, determined not to fall under his spell ever again.

11

The House on the Beach

Greg was beside her before she had time to evade him. He tried to take her hand and looked puzzled when she wouldn't let him. Then his smile turned to a frown. 'Carrie, what's the matter? Why have you been so long?'

She scowled at him. 'I don't want to talk to you. If you'll let me get to reception I want to deposit my key.'

He drew back in shock. 'Carrie, this is ridiculous. Why are you acting like this?'

She looked him straight in the eye. 'I don't know what sort of game you think you're playing, but I want nothing to do with it. I'm going on a coach trip this afternoon and I'm late already.'

He took her arm. 'No, you're not.

Not until you've told me what this is about.'

She shook him off and tried to move towards the desk. People were beginning to look at them.

Greg barred her way. 'Carrie, we can go over into that corner and talk quietly. Or you can fight me here in public. But I will not let you leave until I get to the bottom of this.'

She turned and walked over to the small area off reception that he was indicating. Creating a disturbance was the last thing she wanted. And she needed to sit down. Her reserves were low. She hadn't any fight left in her.

She perched on the edge of the leather settee, just wanting to get this over with, all thought of the market trip put out of mind. He sat opposite, never taking his eyes from her. But she was determined not to let him get to her again. She'd missed the coach now but it didn't matter. Nothing seemed to matter anymore.

'Now tell me what you're talking

about,' Greg demanded.

She sat mute, trying not to wilt under his penetrating gaze.

He was becoming angrier. 'Why weren't you at the house? When I got home late last night and you weren't there, I thought you'd decided to go home.'

Finally she found her tongue. 'So why are you here?'

'Because when I saw the blinds were up and the lounger was in the middle of the lawn, I knew you'd been there. There was no trace of your things in the house, so I guessed you'd decided to stay on at the hotel.' His expression softened as he looked deep into her eyes. 'Carrie, speak to me. Tell me what all this is about.'

It took all her willpower to resist that look, but she knew she had to stay strong and not let him win her over again with his charm. 'It's about me going to your house and finding your lady friend installed there.'

There was a shift in his expression

and the colour drained from his face. 'Renée was there?'

'I didn't get her name. She was too busy warning me off you. Well, she's welcome to you. I can't believe I've been such a fool.'

He was becoming more anguished. 'What has Renée done to upset you?'

She took a deep breath, wanting to get this over with as quickly as possible before she buckled under the emotions that he was again stirring up in her. 'I went to your house yesterday and she was in the garden sunbathing. I asked her who she was and she told me.'

He stood up abruptly. 'She had no business to be there. I don't know why she was there. So what did she tell you?'

She looked up at him and, by summoning every ounce of willpower she possessed, kept her gaze steady. 'She told me you'd lived in the house together until you locked her out.'

His expression hardened. 'Carrie, if you think I'd do such a thing then you might as well go off to the airport and fly home.'

'Well, what's your version of it?' she snapped back.

'I don't have a version of it. But I'll tell you what the situation is.'

She continued to hold his gaze. 'Good, go ahead. This should be interesting.'

Slowly he eased himself back onto the edge of the seat opposite her and hesitated for a moment, his expression becoming more composed. 'We lived together for a couple of years in my apartment. When that house came on the market, she persuaded me to buy it against my better judgement. She wasn't happy with me being away, and I thought it would please her; make up for the fact that I wasn't home much, and give her a project.'

'Okay, I don't need your life story,' Carrie snapped. She wasn't in the mood for this conversation.

He gave a sigh of exasperation. 'Carrie, please. Just let me finish.' She pursed her lips tightly and he continued. 'The house was very rundown. She did get it looking beautiful. But it was my money she used, and she was the one who wanted to do it. I was happy with the small apartment I lived in before I met her. But she wasn't content with that. Nothing was ever enough.'

Carrie got up. She didn't want to hear about this woman and their life together.

He was on his feet and beside her immediately. 'Carrie, I'm trying to explain. Please.'

'Greg, I'm not interested in your life with this Renée. I just want you to leave me alone.'

'But maybe if you listen to me you won't want that.'

He tried to take her arm to stop her but she quickly moved out of reach and faced him full on.

'Greg, nothing you can say can change the fact that you have another woman in your life. I'm not competing with her.'

He moved towards her, and this time she didn't flinch as he took her firmly by the shoulders. The intensity of his look silenced her.

'Carrie, listen to me. I do not have another woman in my life. Renée and I were finished long ago.'

She longed to believe him but no longer trusted her own judgement.

His fingers were digging into her shoulders, his eyes burning. 'She tried to get me to give up my job. I wouldn't. It's the one thing I will never give up for anyone. So she left me. She went back to live in her own house, one much grander than mine, the one she managed to secure for herself when she divorced her husband. She's now living there with the new man in her life. She has no claim on my house, whatever she may think, and there is no way she is going to waltz in and out at her pleasure. That's why I changed the locks.' He dropped his hands from her shoulders but still held her gaze, his expression challenging.

She felt her insides churning. 'Are you married to her?'

His eyes widened. 'Do you really think I'd be standing here trying to persuade you to stay with me if I was married?'

She shook her head miserably as she began to realise he was speaking the truth — that everything he was telling her made sense, and she had jumped to conclusions too quickly and misjudged him.

His expression relaxed and his voice became more conciliatory. 'Carrie, my life doesn't lend itself to marriage. I'm away more than I'm home.'

'I'm sorry,' she mumbled, looking down.

He moved closer and lifted her chin so that she was forced to look him in the eye, his expression now tender. 'And I'm sorry you've had such a terrible experience.'

She tried to turn away, not knowing what to say. But he wouldn't let her. 'Carrie, do you believe me?'

She felt herself slump, totally deflated. She'd got it all wrong and now there was no going back. She'd shown him that she didn't trust him; had listened to that woman and let it spoil everything they could have had.

She nodded. 'I better get on my way.'

His jaw tensed. 'My car's outside. I can take you anywhere you want to go.'

'No, I'll find my own way,' she said quietly.

'Is that what you want?'

She shook her head as tears overflowed and ran down her cheeks.

'Carrie,' he said gently but firmly, 'I need to know.' His words hung in the air. 'Carrie?' he said again. He was studying her keenly.

She swallowed. 'I don't want us to part like this.'

'Then why are you going?' His voice was hardly more than a whisper.

She turned her tear-stained face towards him. 'Because I've messed up.'

His expression relaxed slightly. 'We both have.'

She stood looking up at him, trying desperately to stop shaking.

'I don't want you to go,' he said.

'I don't want to,' she whispered.

They stared at each other as he took both her hands in his. Then he pulled her close, and as his arms enfolded her she relaxed into him. Very gently his lips touched hers, and she let his kiss banish all the doubt and anguish from her mind.

Carrie had no idea how long they had stood in that embrace in the middle of the reception area of the busy hotel, nor did she care. Her heart was full of love and gratitude that Greg had not let her make the biggest mistake of her life and that he felt enough for her to forgive her stupidity.

He gave his car keys to the concierge, and within minutes the vehicle was parked outside the hotel entrance. As they sped along the seafront, he glanced at Carrie. 'You look worried. I'm not taking you back to the house. I know you wouldn't want that.'

'Where are we going?' She really didn't care where he was taking her. Being with him was enough.

'A lovely little house on the beach. Belongs to a friend of mine. He's cruising the Bahamas on his ship at the moment. I use his house when he's away.'

Carrie felt a sudden joyful anticipation of the week ahead. 'Why are you using your friend's house?'

He glanced at her, a broad smile lighting up his face. 'Because it's closer to your hotel and I want to spend every moment of the next week with you.'

Greg stopped the car outside a lovely little whitewashed cottage, not quite on the beach but nestled into the hillside with a view out across the bay. He silenced the engine and turned to her. 'And I don't like that house on the island any more than you do.'

As soon as Carrie stepped inside the cottage, she felt at home. It was small and cosy, with wooden beams and a fireplace with logs set ready to light.

Greg took her in his arms and held her as if he would never let her go. He smelt of aftershave and something distinctive that was just Greg. The touch of his lips was gentle at first; and then, as his kisses became more urgent, the world fell away and Carrie was lost in the moment.

Finally he loosened his hold on her. 'Happy?' he murmured into her hair.

She leaned back so that she could see his face, her arms still round his neck, love and longing surging through her.

'Carrie, I wouldn't do anything to hurt you.'

'I'm sorry. I should have trusted you.'

He tweaked her nose and gave her a roguish grin. 'Yes, you should.'

She rested her head against his chest as he pulled her close.

* * *

They spent the afternoon wandering along the seashore, sitting occasionally on long tree trunks scattered here and there on the sand. Carrie explained how Tom had looked after her when they had left the ship and how much she had appreciated his company. Greg didn't comment, and she worried that he thought she and Tom were more than friends. But he didn't seem disturbed by the conversation.

She told him about her brother Neil and his wife, and how she adored her niece and nephew. They didn't talk about her plans for working with Julia at the dancing school when she got home. It would have spoiled the moment.

He told her more about his disastrous relationship with Renée. She had wanted marriage but he had been reluctant, not having had good experiences of relationships in the past. And he was glad now, because it would have been more difficult to split up when she'd left.

'It is a lovely house,' Carrie ventured. 'But why do you keep all your paintings in that tiny room?'

He huffed. 'It was Renée. She thought they would spoil the decor. She liked the minimalist look — everything like a show house. That tiny room was my den, the only bit of the house I felt at home in. She even resented the time I spent painting because I wasn't paying attention to her.'

Carrie squeezed his hand to show she understood, but said nothing. She didn't feel she should comment on this relationship she knew little of.

Later they found a small fish restaurant to eat in. When they came out, the sky was a blaze of colour. The air smelled of seaweed and wood smoke. Golden flames rose from the beach where groups of youngsters sat round on logs, their faces bright with firelight, laughing and talking, some holding each other close as they enjoyed the balmy night. Barbeque smells rose in the air. Someone began to play a guitar and others gathered round him swaying and singing, their voices drifting through the night air.

Carrie stood close to Greg, absorbing all this happiness and wishing with all her heart that it could last.

All along the promenade people were strolling, lovers in each other's arms. Brightly lit skyscrapers dazzled the eye and, when they stopped to look out over the sea, Carrie felt her heart would burst with happiness as she watched the sun drop low behind the dark mountains and colour the sky with a deep vermilion. Greg put his arm round her waist and she smiled to herself, content just to be with him for these few days.

It was only when she was alone in her hotel room once more that a sadness fell over her. They'd talked of their lives, and it had brought home to her how short their time together was going to be. She'd decided it would be worth the eventual pain of parting, but she hadn't planned on her feelings for him growing so strong so quickly.

If only she could stay and be with him always. But it was an impossible dream. She had her life back home. He had his ship. He didn't want commitment; he'd made that very clear. She just had to enjoy the moment. Holiday romances never lasted. At least she would have some happy memories to take home with her.

⋆ ⋆ ⋆

Greg was at the hotel first thing the next morning to pick her up, looking effortlessly handsome in well-fitting trousers, his skin dark against his pale blue shirt. Soon they were driving over the Lions Gate Bridge and into Stanley Park, a huge open space on the outskirts of the city very close to the sea. A couple of galloping horses nearly trampled them down when they mistook a bridleway for a walkway. Swimmers splashed around in one of the lakes and Carrie wished she could join them. The day was getting hotter as the sun rose high in a cloudless sky.

'I love Vancouver,' she said as they strolled along the pathways between shady trees and took in the fresh sea air.

Greg stopped and turned to look at her. 'I'm surprised you didn't take off in shock after what happened.'

'I nearly did. It was Tom who calmed me down. In fact it was Tom who told me to stay in the first place.'

He put an arm round her waist and pulled her close. 'Tom's a very generous man. He was in love with you, you know. But he understood. He knew how I felt about you and he seemed to think you felt the same way. Was he right, Carrie?'

She looked away, embarrassed. 'I'm not sure how I feel about you, Greg. That's why I stayed.'

He waited until she was forced to look back at him, and then he gave her a mischievous smile. 'Well, I'd better be on my best behaviour, then.'

They strolled through the trees and onto a path that followed the coastline. 'I'm always happiest when I can see the sea,' Greg said. 'I don't think I could live inland.'

'You wouldn't be happy where I live then,' she laughed. 'You couldn't get any further away from it.'

'I don't think I'd be too unhappy if you were around,' he said, squeezing her hand, and Carrie felt a lightness in her step.

As they continued to walk, he became more serious. 'Did you know Heidi's left the ship?'

'She told me she intended to, but I thought she was just having a bad day.'

'Well, she's gone, and they need to replace her.' He paused, and without looking at her said, 'You know what I'm thinking, don't you?'

Carrie kept her eyes firmly on the path ahead and tried to sound matter-of-fact. 'Brett did ask me when I was on the ship. He seemed to know then that she'd be leaving.'

'And how do you feel about it?'

She shook her head. 'I couldn't do it.'

He took her hand then and moved in front of her, stopping her progress. 'Carrie, you could. You'd be perfect.

You dance beautifully. You get on well with Brett. You're good with people. So what's the problem?'

Her stomach began to churn. 'Is that why you asked me to stay?'

'I suppose it was in the back of my mind,' he said.

Happiness drained from her as the meaning of his words sunk in. He wasn't interested in her. He just wanted to fill the job.

'And I want you with me,' he said hurriedly as if reading her thoughts.

'But why?' she said, now totally confused.

He took both her hands in his and looked deep into her eyes. 'You know that very well.' He stood uncertainly in front of her, waiting.

She took a deep breath, knowing she had to be strong. She really did not know what he was offering, if anything at all. If she fell under his spell now, she would be lost.

'Greg, I have a home in England. My family are there, and I already have a job. I can't drop everything on a whim.'

A shadow passed over his face. 'I see.'

They began to walk again, an uncomfortable silence hanging between them. Back in the park they found a large collection of totem poles and tried to work out the stories they told in an effort to lighten their mood.

'Tom knew all about totem poles and what they stood for,' Carrie offered with a smile as the tension between them eased.

'Right — come on then, you can tell me.'

She laughed. 'No chance. I can't remember any of it, only that they're part of the First Nations culture. I think he felt a bit embarrassed. He put his book away when I gave him a blank look.'

Greg threw his head back and laughed. 'You heartless woman. Poor old Tom.'

Carrie fell silent. She shouldn't be joking about Tom. He was a good friend and had supported her through all her bad days. She wouldn't be here with Greg now if it hadn't been for him.

Greg noticed. 'I liked Tom. There aren't many of his type around these days. Will you see him again when you go home?'

So he'd accepted that she was going home. He obviously wasn't going to try to persuade her otherwise. And why should he? He'd offered her the chance to stay so they could get to know each other better. She'd made it obvious it wasn't something she was prepared to do. Yet her heart plummeted at his acceptance of the situation. All she could manage was a nod. He took her hand and they carried on walking.

Staring out to sea at Prospect Point, Carrie suddenly jumped as something scuttled past her and she saw a racoon disappear into the bushes.

Greg laughed. 'Don't suppose you get many of those running around in your garden.'

The gloom that had engulfed them

was again temporarily banished.

That evening they ate an Oriental meal in a little café in the town and emerged as the sun was setting behind the dark silhouette of the mountains, turning the sky ablaze with streaks of crimson. Carrie loved this time of day, with the promenade transformed into a fairyland of illuminated buildings that rose high into the sky. As they wandered along, Greg with his arm loosely round her waist, she had never felt so fulfilled.

Back in the little house they sat talking into the early hours, each hungry for knowledge of the other, content just being together. Flames from the fire lit up the old timber beams, and the candles Greg had lit gave out a relaxing aroma. Gentle music filtered through the speakers as they cuddled up together on the old sofa. Through the window the sky was bright with stars, and a crescent moon filled one tiny pane of glass.

Greg told Carrie about his childhood

moving from place to place when his father was in the army, and how he had finally been sent to boarding school in England.

'How come you live in Vancouver?' Carrie asked.

'I did my first cruise from Vancouver after joining the company and, as I really didn't have any roots, I decided to make it my home.'

'I can understand why,' Carrie said.

Greg gave her a wistful smile. 'And what about your life? I feel it hasn't been full of fun.'

She shook her head. 'No, not recently.'

'And in the future?' he asked.

'It'll be a challenge. Julia's helped me through some bad times. I'll enjoy working with her.' But as she spoke she could hear the flatness in her own voice. The enthusiasm she had felt only weeks ago seemed to have disappeared overnight. Going back home and teaching children to tap dance and old people to sequence dance didn't have the allure it once did.

'You dance so beautifully. It's when I fell in love with you. Did you know that? When I saw you doing that rumba out on deck on the last night with Brett. You looked so radiant in your long emerald dress.'

Had he just said he loved her? She stared at him, unable to believe what she was hearing. Despite her best intentions, a surge of excitement shot through her. Quickly she turned away, not wanting him to see how much his words had affected her. He did have feelings for her. Feelings that matched her own. But she couldn't afford to have these feelings. She had to remind herself that he didn't want commitment. He hadn't offered anything other than the opportunity to take a job on his ship.

'The dance of love. Yes, it's my favourite dance. It's so sensual,' she said, moving slightly away from him.

He didn't comment, but released her from his arms and stretched as if in resignation. 'And will this satisfy you? Teaching children to dance, I mean. It seems like wasting a lot of talent.'

'I have to earn a living.'

He was looking at her intently. 'Don't you want a family of your own? Children?'

She shrugged. 'That isn't something you can have to order.'

'No,' he said.

Carrie frowned. 'And you, Greg, I hardly know anything about your relationships. Only Renée.'

He took a deep breath. 'I've had my share. Usually lasting only the length of one leave. It just hasn't happened for me.'

'And children. Would you like them?'

His expression softened. 'Of course. That's my one regret. But you have to have the right relationship before you bring children into it. And my job doesn't allow for that.'

She sighed. 'I have my niece and nephew.'

'Not the same, though, is it?'

'There's no point in regrets. We have to get on with what we can have.'

He shook his head. 'I don't think that's always a good thing.'

She looked questioningly at him.

He took her hand. 'Carrie, I think you want much more than that.'

She shrugged. 'Maybe.'

The light was fading, but it was still strong enough for her to search his eyes. She found sadness and regret there.

'Carrie, will you think about taking Heidi's place on the ship? Ballroom dancing is so popular on cruises. You'd have Brett for a partner, and you could give lessons and demonstrations.' He hesitated. 'And it would give us a little more time together.'

Her heart sank. A little more time was all he wanted. 'And then what? Look at Sally and Rob. And Heidi.'

He nodded. 'You're right, there are no guarantees. It's a precarious life working on a cruise ship. I can't promise anything.'

He'd admitted it. She knew she couldn't safely put her life in this man's hands. She had to stick to her plan and go home.

'I can't take that risk, Greg. I don't want any more heartache. I just want a settled life.'

He nodded. 'I know.'

He got up, pulled her from the sofa and took her in his arms as an unknown voice from the radio was singing about dreaming dreams. Neither spoke. They just held each other tight, knowing this would be all they would ever have.

* * *

Back in the hotel alone, Carrie had time to think about their conversation. Greg had said he loved her. But that didn't mean he wanted to spend his life with her. In fact, he had told her in so many words that he could make no such commitment. Simon, too, had said he loved her, and that hadn't meant much in the end. No, Greg's life was on his ship. He'd had too many failed relationships to trust love. And she could understand that. The hurt when a relationship broke up was unbearably sad. No, her best chance of happiness was to go home.

12

The Last Dance

Their time together passed too quickly. It was to be their last day before Greg was due back on his ship and Carrie would fly home. She was up early, and with a heavy heart began to pack. It had been an emotional week — the happiest she could remember, and the most painful. And now it was to come to a close. Tomorrow evening she would be home, and Greg would be up on the bridge again with another ship full of passengers. Before long all this would be a distant memory.

With just enough clothes left out for the day, she closed the lid of her case. At least it was ready for take-off tomorrow. She didn't want to waste a moment of the time they had left.

Greg had business to attend to and

was gone longer than she'd expected. When he arrived at the hotel to pick her up, he seemed subdued. He kissed her tenderly, then took her hand. 'I have a special afternoon planned for you,' he said, forcing a smile.

She was glad they were going to keep occupied, as it would help them not to mope.

They drove off and were soon high in the mountains amongst stunning beauty. Greg parked the car and guided Carrie along a path through huge trees towards a great canyon with a long rickety bridge suspended across it.

'We're not going to walk over that,' she said in alarm.

He laughed. 'It's quite safe, I can assure you.'

It gave her a giddy feeling being suspended thousands of feet in the air. She gripped Greg's hand as the bridge began to wobble.

He laughed. 'Kids fooling around. They're not supposed to jump around on it but they always do.'

Once on the other side, they climbed up to a raised boardwalk high up among the ancient cedars, then back across the bridge to the car.

The next stop was Grouse Mountain, where they took a chair lift to the top and saw lumberjacks performing breath-taking acrobatics at dizzying heights. In the enclosure where they kept rescued bears, only one was visible, and he was lying behind a tree.

'Come on, bear, wake up! I want to see you,' Carrie whispered.

Greg put an arm round her shoulders. 'He's having a siesta. Don't disturb him.'

She gave a pretend pout. 'Well, he could just give us a friendly paw-wave, since we've come all this way to see him.'

'Come on, he's not going to oblige. Let's find somewhere to sit down.'

They found a grassy bank with a spectacular view down the mountain and sat on the ground, watching deer further down the slope munching the vegetation. Greg took Carrie's hand, and there was sadness in his eyes. 'Carrie, I wish you weren't leaving tomorrow.'

She could hardly speak, her throat was so tight. 'I have to. I can't stay here. You'll be off on your ship again tomorrow and I'll be on my flight home.'

'Are you really set on this dancing school venture?' he asked.

'Yes,' she said. 'It's a fresh start. Julia thinks we'll be able to rent another studio and start up new classes, expand the whole business. We plan to put on two shows a year now, one in the summer and one at Christmas.' She had to keep talking about it. She had to keep reassuring herself it was what she wanted. She couldn't let herself be persuaded to stay. She couldn't go through all that pain again if it didn't work out.

Greg was watching her intently. 'But is it what you really want?'

'Yes,' she said firmly. 'I've promised

Julia I'll be there on Monday ready to start. I can't put her off any longer.'

A sadness crept over his face. 'Our relationship means a lot to me. You know that, don't you?'

She turned away. A lot wasn't enough.

'You're afraid of being hurt again?' he said gently.

'Yes.'

'And I'm afraid too.'

She began to realise his feelings ran deep. But she mustn't let herself be drawn in. It was too dangerous. Teaching was safe. It was something she could do, something she wouldn't fail at. She had to get on that plane and get back home. Neil and his family would never let her down. Julia would never let her down. Love did.

She was so absorbed in her thoughts that she hadn't realised Greg was still talking softly to her. 'When I saw you dancing with Brett,' he said, 'I saw the real Carrie, confident and happy. I wanted you to be like that always. And I wanted it to be because you were with me.' She quickly pulled herself together and gave him a weak smile. He didn't return it. 'I was unbearably jealous. I couldn't stand to see you in someone else's arms. I ached to have you in mine.'

She rested her head on his shoulder and he pulled her to him. They were quiet for a moment, his warmth comforting.

'I think you want to be with me as much as I want to be with you,' he almost whispered, looking out across the mountains. He was waiting for an answer.

'It's not possible, Greg.'

Suddenly he sprang to his feet, tense and anxious. 'Carrie, it *is* possible. Why won't you stay and come on the ship with me? Even if it was only for a couple of years. There would be plenty of time after that to settle down. In the meantime you can see the world, travel, dance, have some fun.'

She stared up at him, alarmed at his

change of mood. He pulled her to her feet and held her so tight she could hardly breathe. Then he put her away from him and gave her a pleading look. 'Please, Carrie.'

When she didn't respond, his grip on her slackened and his face sank into despair. It almost broke her heart to see him like this. She longed to tell him how much she loved him and that she would do anything to stay near him. All her senses were screaming at her to take this opportunity he was offering, but her mind was telling her not to be a fool.

'Come on, let's get back. We've both got a long day ahead tomorrow,' she managed.

Now that it had got to this stage, she really wanted to get it all over with. She knew the final goodbye was going to tear her apart. But work was her goal now, and carving out a successful future. Her career was about to take off. She was finally free. No more loyalty to anyone. That way she could stay in control of her life.

They hardly spoke on the drive back. Greg didn't go into the hotel with Carrie, but dropped her off outside the entrance. Neither spoke, but their eyes, when they met, said it all. She rushed up the steps and inside as quickly as she could and didn't look back. Then she got in the lift, went straight to her room, and flung herself onto the bed face down with a feeling of total and utter despair.

★　★　★

By three o'clock in the morning Carrie was still tossing in bed, her mind in turmoil. Every bit of her was aching with love and longing and pain. She'd been through every emotion and every argument in her head. She loved Greg — there was no denying it. He'd said he loved her. They wanted to be together. She dreaded going home to her lonely house. She'd lost all enthusiasm for the dancing school. She didn't want to teach children to dance. She didn't want any part of her old life, on her own, relying on her brother and his family for comfort. Growing old, fussing over his children because she had no children of her own to love. Always being on the outside, looking in. But was it crazy to abandon the security of the tried and tested for the uncertainty of the unknown?

Then she'd remember that Greg had said he didn't want commitment; had told her his life didn't lend itself to a steady relationship. If she stayed to be with him, what sort of a future could she look forward to? If Greg was transferred to another ship and they didn't want her, what then? She'd be on her own in a foreign country, with no friends or family.

If he rejected her, she knew it would devastate her. She must never let herself get into that position again. If she went home, she'd have her family for support. She'd be working with her best friend. She would have security.

Or she could take a chance on happiness. Should she listen to the voice of caution? Or follow her heart and reach out for love? If she didn't take this chance, every part of her life from now on would have to be lived with regret. Without the man she loved.

She tossed and turned in the bed. Her stomach was churning and she couldn't sleep. She reached out to the radio. Some gentle music might help. She lay back on her pillow and tried to let her mind drift.

First Ella was crooning about this thing called love. Carrie wasn't sure it was really helping, but just making her want Greg more than ever. Then she was listening to that beautiful song about memories, about being all alone in the moonlight. Tears were pouring down her face until she felt she could bear it no longer. She was aching with longing and loneliness. She didn't want memories. She wanted Greg.

She sat bolt upright in bed and picked up the phone. He answered immediately. 'I need to talk,' she said.

'I'll pick you up in ten minutes. Wait in the foyer.'

'I'll be there.'

They drove back to the little house on the beach in silence. Inside, Greg took Carrie in his arms and hugged her to him. 'I can't go,' she mumbled into his chest.

He was silent and just held her to him. When he still didn't speak, she lifted her head and looked into his eyes. His face was contorted with misery.

Eventually he managed to speak, but only in a whisper. 'Carrie, I can't ask you to stay.'

Her mouth opened in a silent gasp as she placed a hand against his shoulder and leaned back to look into his face, not comprehending what he was telling her. Shock prevented her from speaking immediately.

Finally she found her voice. 'But you said this afternoon — '

'I know.'

She had never experienced so much

pain. He'd changed his mind. Her worst fears had been realised. 'Then why did you bring me here?' she asked, her voice hardly audible.

He swallowed hard. 'Because I wanted to be with you one last time.'

She blinked in bewilderment, hardly able to take this in, her heart beating erratically. 'But you told me you wanted me to stay so we could be together.' She dropped her arms from round his neck and eased herself into the big armchair behind her and covered her face with her hands.

He crouched in front of her and gently drew them away. 'Carrie, I love you.'

'Then why have you changed your mind?' she whispered through tight lips.

'Because I could see it wasn't right for you. You didn't want to give up your life at home for the life I was offering.'

'But I do now.' It came out as a sob.

He gave a long, low sigh. 'Sometimes I'm away for months on end. I can't give up the life I know and love.'

'I would never ask you to do that. I love you. I wouldn't want you to change in any way.'

'But what about you? You have a whole future mapped out for you. You've got friends and family in England, a home, challenging work. Why would you leave all that to sit at home here, waiting for me while I'm away doing what I enjoy?'

'I'll take the job on the ship,' she gasped.

He shook his head. 'No, you don't want the job. You'd be taking it just to be with me.'

'But that *is* what I want; I want to be with you,' she almost wailed in frustration.

'But I can't promise we can always be together.'

She stared at him mutely, unable to form any more words. She'd never felt such pain. All the time he held her hands, an anguished look distorting his face.

'Carrie, it won't work.' His clipped

voice told her how difficult this was for him.

'If you loved me enough it could work,' she managed eventually, a break in her voice. The thought of losing him had become unbearable.

He was squeezing her hands tightly, his eyes full of compassion.

'Greg, if we part now I'll never see you again. Whatever time we could have together must be better than that,' she sobbed.

He regarded her steadily. 'No, it wouldn't.'

So this was it. She should have known. She should have listened to her own caution. He wasn't going to make any commitment. He'd told her many times that he couldn't. He wasn't prepared to give up his freedom. If he thought so little of her, there was no point in her staying.

She got up stiffly and somehow managed to make it to the door, her legs like jelly, her whole body shaking uncontrollably. Leaning her face onto the hard surface of the wall, she drew her fists up and hammered them into it. He came up behind her, and she could feel his eyes burning into her back as anger and hurt were raging through her.

'Go away,' she said, her voice frighteningly calm. Then she turned to him as he stood in front of her, eyes blazing. 'Why do you torment me like this? One minute pleading with me to stay. Then you turn me aside, telling me to go. Why, Greg, why?'

After what seemed like forever, he held out his hands towards her. They were trembling. 'Carrie, I don't want you to go.'

At once her anger was gone. She reached out to him, hardly daring to breathe while she waited for him to speak. His expression changed as if he'd made a decision.

Taking a few steps closer, he took both her hands in his. 'Do you really think we can make it work?' The tightness in his voice told her how much the words were costing him.

Her relief was overwhelming. She hadn't known until this minute quite how much she had feared losing him. She started to speak but he drew her to him and, holding her trembling body, put a finger to her lips. 'Think about it, Carrie. Think really carefully. I couldn't bear for you to be unhappy because of me.'

He was looking at her intently, concern etched on his face. He was waiting for her answer.

'I've thought about nothing else for days,' she whispered.

'And me.'

A bubble of hope was rising inside her. 'It can work if we both want it to. But I'm not sure how much you want it.'

He took a deep breath. 'I want it more than anything.'

She looked deep into his eyes. 'Then why are you so uncertain?'

'Because you have such a lot to give up to stay here with me. Do you really want to do that?'

'I would do anything to be with you.' She was surprised at how steady her voice had become.

He drew her closer, and warmth spread through her as she lifted her arms round his neck, now feeling safe in the circle of his love.

'I made a decision just then,' he said. 'About something I never thought I could do.'

She held her breath as she waited for him to continue.

He hesitated and cleared his throat. 'If I have to change my life, I will, because I love you too much to let you go. I never thought I'd want anything enough to do that. But now I do.'

Her heart was beating wildly. He loved her that much! 'I've told you I'd never ask you to do that.' She wanted to reassure him that her love was unconditional.

A smile was breaking on his face. 'You wouldn't have to.'

'Greg, I'm not Renée.'

He winced. 'I know. But what about Julia? You'll be letting her down.'

She shook her head. 'She'll understand. She's always telling me I have to think about my own life now, and do what I feel is right for me.'

'And is this right for you?'

'Yes, Greg. I've never been so sure of anything in my life.'

He stood back and looked at her as if trying to believe she meant it. Then he was hugging her so tight she couldn't breathe. As their lips met, she knew with certainty that she never wanted to be anywhere other than with this man, no matter what lay ahead.

★ ★ ★

The sky was lightening as they sat together curled up on the old sofa in front of the dying embers of the fire, discussing their future.

'Are you sure I can have the job?' Carrie asked, suddenly wondering if Greg could fix it so easily.

He shrugged. 'There are a few formalities we have to go through. But from what you've told me, you have all the qualifications. There shouldn't be a problem.' Then he was grinning. 'I'll have to keep an eye on you and Brett.'

She frowned. 'You won't be jealous every time you see me dancing with him, will you?'

'I'll always be jealous of anyone who holds you in their arms. But so long as you save the last dance for me, I think I'll be able to cope.' He was thoughtful. 'I'll never forget the feelings I had when I watched you dance that rumba with him. It was the way you looked at him.'

'Greg, it was a dance. The dance of love. You have to put some emotion into it. It's what makes it so special.'

A ghost of a smile touched his lips. 'I know that now.' Then, getting to his feet, he said, 'I have to go. We sail in a few hours' time. And you have to let them know you're not travelling home on that flight today.'

Carrie got up and stood with him. 'I

have to find somewhere to live. I have some savings, but not enough to keep me for long, not until I've sold my house.'

He gave her a bemused look. 'I have enough for both of us. And you can stay here.'

She shook her head furiously. 'No, that wouldn't be right. I don't even know this friend of yours. I'd feel like I was trespassing.'

He cast her a tolerant glance. 'You're making difficulties where they don't exist.'

'But I can't let you keep me.'

He drew his hand though his hair and gave her an exasperated look. 'So what's the answer?'

She shook her head and gave him a doleful look. 'I don't know.'

He paused and a mischievous smile crossed his face. 'Once we're married, I hope you'll be living with me.'

She stared at him. 'You haven't asked me to marry you.'

A shadow passed over his face. 'Do I have to?'

Sheer joy was bubbling up inside her, making her feel light-headed and giddy. 'You are so arrogant,' she said, confident of his love now and determined to take pleasure in teasing him.

He backed away. 'What have I done now?'

'You think you just have to snap your fingers and everyone does exactly as you want them to.' It was becoming harder to keep a straight face, but she was enjoying the moment, watching his normal confidence challenged. But also knowing that he knew what her answer would be.

He shrugged. 'They usually do.'

'Well, I don't.' It was difficult to sound cross when she was brimming over with happiness.

Then he looked at her uncertainly. 'Would that be a no, then? If I did ask you, that is?'

She realised he wasn't so sure at all. She reached up to hug him to her. 'Why not try me?'

He knelt down on one knee, looked

into her eyes and took her hand. 'Carrie Davis, would you do me the honour of becoming my wife?'

She felt her heart bursting with happiness. Then tears began to roll down her cheeks.

He was quickly on his feet. 'Carrie, what is it now?'

She tried to smile, then buried her face in his chest until she could gain some composure. Then she lifted her face to him. 'Yes,' she gulped.

He let out a long breath. 'Not quite the reaction I expected. You had me worried there for a while.'

The strains of 'What a Difference a Day Makes' drifted from the radio as they swayed together. Then she pulled away from him.

'Greg, I have to tell Julia.'

He nodded and left the room to collect his gear together while she dialled the number. Her hands were trembling while she waited for Julia to pick up.

'Julia, I've decided to stay,' she said,

gripping the phone tight.

There was a squeal from the other end. 'I'm so pleased for you.'

Carrie felt a lump forming in her throat, making it difficult to speak. But it didn't matter; Julia was in full flow. 'When can I come and see you? I can't wait to set eyes on this gorgeous man.'

Eventually Carrie managed to answer all Julia's questions and to reassure her she would always be welcome as a guest anytime. When the phone went dead she sat with it in her hand, staring at it until Greg came back into the room, dressed in his uniform and ready to go. He put the small grip he was carrying down on the table and took the phone from Carrie's hand.

'I'll phone Tom later,' she said in a small voice.

'You'll see him again soon,' Greg said.

She looked up at him through eyes brimming with unshed tears.

'He'll come to our wedding,' Greg told her gently.

311

She frowned. 'How can you be so sure?'

He gave her one of his heart-stopping smiles. 'Because I'm going to ask him to be my best man.'

'But you hardly know him.'

'I know that without Tom there wouldn't be a wedding.'

Carrie felt her eyes filling up and squeezed them tight.

'I have to go,' Greg said. 'They can't sail without me.'

She managed a watery smile. 'Go then. I have a lot to organise.'

'Soon there'll be no more goodbyes. The company never separate married couples.'

She frowned. 'That's not why you asked me to marry you, is it?'

He gave her a despairing look. 'I asked you to marry me because I love you and I want to spend the rest of my life with you. Now stop all this nonsense.'

She tried to look suitably rebuked, but her heart was bursting with joy.

'Carrie, stop doubting me. You'll be on that ship as soon as it can be arranged. Then we'll never be separated again.'

'While there are only two of us.' The words were out before she'd thought.

But his smile was breaking into a grin that spread across his face. 'Then we'll both have to rethink our careers.'

'But you always said — '

He put a finger to her lips to silence her. 'We're in this together. Everything's different now that I've found you. I love you, Carrie, and that love will always come first.'

A feeling of pure joy spread through her as the future suddenly held a promise of everything she had ever wished for. Their plans would change over the years. She would never expect more of him than he could give, but the fact that he was willing to change his whole way of life for her was all she needed. His love was unconditional, and so was hers, and she knew for certain she had made the right decision.

Happiness threatened to overflow as he took her in his arms. Reluctantly he drew away, his eyes still holding hers. 'Remember, my love, the last dance should last forever.'

And she knew it would.